Lines of Force

Weekend
The ^ Adventures of Andrew Barton

Drew Bankston

OldStache Publishing

Greeley, Colorado

ISBN 979-8-9897381-0-6
http://www.drewbankston.com

Cover design by Christi Bankston

Printed in the United States of America

Dedication

I dedicate this book to my family, who share me generously with my computer at all hours of the day and night, and to the inventor spirit that resides in us all!

-Drew.

CHAPTER 1

Time to Spare

Dedicated to the people who spend their lives researching and developing their ideas. Those who have made many significant discoveries in their time. Several of those people never get to see the end results of their labors. Sometimes, very often, discoveries are made purely by accident. Many of them change the world and the people that live in it. Some benefit only a few people. Others affect one person and, in small ways unbeknownst to the world, affect every living being in one way or another. This is the story of one man who accidentally stumbled upon things that most of us only dream about. ~ Andrew Barton

"My name is Andrew Barton, but you can call me Andrew. Everyone has for as long as I can remember, which isn't long compared to other things in this world. I, like many other people, went to college. A fairly good college, as a matter of fact. I studied Agricultural Sciences and worked in that field for about three years until the bottom dropped out of my specialty. It was then that I had to find other avenues of employment. Fortunately for me, a world-renowned retailer was hiring in my area, and I promptly became a forklift driver at one of their less-than-state-of-the-art warehouses. Not my dream job by any means, but it paid the bills."

"Being the curious soul I am and always interested in science, I found time to tinker in my garage every chance I could. Okay, it was only on weekends, but it was an amazing time. I'm sure this was much to the dismay of my wife, Julie."

"Julie and I have been married for ten years. She's a wonderful woman. She's kind, understanding, pretty, and smart, but best of all, she puts up with me and my little quirks. I'm not sure why she does it, but I'm grateful. She understands me and my need to explore the world around me."

"I don't know how often she's patiently listened to my stories about magnets. I've been fascinated with magnets since I was a kid. They were so cool! Wait, no, they are so cool! Perhaps you can relate. Two pieces of metal that can attract and repel other magnets without using batteries. Strange pieces of metal that, when a wire passes over them, create electricity. I always wondered about these amazing anomalies of nature and knew they had some strange, magical, and mystical force we had yet to explore completely."

"As I grew older, I forgot about the magic of magnets but still thought about them from time to time when I would change the alternator in my car or see one in a toy store. Julie would patiently wait for me to stop playing with them, and our eight-year-old daughter, Stephanie, would huff and puff and throw her head back, becoming limp all over, but still manage to stand upright, like a rag doll with equilibrium. 'Come on, Dad!' she'd exclaim in as whiny a voice as she could get away with. 'Why don't you just buy some magnets and play with them at home?'"

"She didn't realize that by making that suggestion, she had inadvertently started us out on a very long and interesting adventure, which assured me that our entire family's future would be forever filled with excitement."

"I bought the magnets and continued to buy them. First, I bought the toy store varieties, and then I went online and started buying the stronger, natural magnets. I wasn't sure where this all was leading to, but I found out soon enough."

"One Christmas, a relative gave me a plasma ball as a gift. As with many science-type things, I looked at it with awe and wonder, and just for fun, I put a magnet up to the glass while it was on. I was amazed at how the magnetic field affected the electricity inside the plasma ball. I could hear it crackle. I watched it bend and dance to the will of the invisible field that called to it. I realized there must be some connection between these three elements; electricity, magnetism, and plasma. That's where I started getting in trouble. I spent every weekend in my makeshift workshop in the garage, trying to figure out the connection between these three mysteries of nature."

"Spending as much time as I did, I learned through experience and, of course, the occasional book or website, things that I had never known about these strange, natural pieces of rock. Let me tell you my story so you can understand how this all went terribly wrong in an incredibly wonderful way!"

CHAPTER 2

It Begins

Andrew sat at his workbench fiddling with wires, batteries, power supplies, and magnets. The plasma ball was on with a magnetic ring tightly surrounding its' equator. Andrew was oblivious to the buzzing and humming of the electrical equipment. He was lost in his thoughts and blinded by his concentration. He rubbed his tired eyes and looked at the digital clock above his workspace. *Six o'clock already!* he thought. *Time goes by too quickly when I'm out here. At least it's only Saturday. I still have all day tomorrow. I wish I had more time, though.* Andrew reached over to adjust the spark coil sitting toward the back of the bench.

The door leading into the kitchen opened. The smells of a roast in the oven drifted out into the garage, mixing with the smell of solder and burnt wires. Julie, Andrew's wife, stepped out onto the top step leading into the cold garage.

"Andrew?" Julie asked softly. When she received no response, she repeated louder, "Andrew!"

"Yeah?" Andrew replied distractedly, not looking up from the wires he was fiddling with.

"Andrew, Susie, and Matt are here," Julie said.

But Andrew, engrossed in his work, replied with a small, "Mmmm."

Julie sighed and crossed her arms. "Andrew, are you hearing me? Where are you?"

"What?" Andrew looked up at Julie as if she had just popped up from the floor. "I'm sorry, sweetheart. What did you say? I'm a little distracted."

"A little?" Julie laughed. "I would say that you were lost in another dimension. I've been standing here for a good five minutes trying to get your attention. Next time, I'll come out in my nightgown and see if that helps."

"Then I would be distracted in another way," Andrew grinned.

"So," Julie said as she started looking over Andrew's workbench, "what's distracting you from me tonight?"

"I'm working on boosting the power I need to run my plasmatic drive," he said. "At least, I'm hoping I can figure this thing out. According to the current laws of physics, this shouldn't be possible, but I've seen those laws change so much over the past few years. Who's to say that I can't create a new one?"

Julie looked at Andrew like she did at their daughter when she was babbling and carrying on with childish nonsense, and shook her head. "You're always working on something or other that's exciting. I'm not sure what the drive is you're working on, but our friends are here to visit. You might think about taking a break and coming inside for a bit. They would love to see you."

"Okay," Andrew sighed, "I'll be in shortly. If I can get this plasmatic drive up and running, it will change how we get around," Andrew said excitedly. His eyes grew wide, and his hands began to explain his words as strongly as they could by flying every which way in front of him. "It's going to be so cool! Gas engines will be a thing of the..."

"Gas engines?" Andrew's friend, Matt Berman, pushed his way past Julie and into the garage, bounding up next to Andrew. Matt was about five foot six and relatively muscular. He was a high school wrestler and went to state in his senior year. He and Andrew had been friends since second grade, and they knew each other almost as well as they knew themselves. "You're working on gas engines? These don't look like any gas engines I've ever seen." He looked over the workbench and began reaching out to fiddle with various objects. Andrew did his best to stop him, but Matt was quick and unpredictable. Finally, Matt grabbed a long, thin tube with a wire attached to one end. He started examining the object and waved it around like a sword. Andrew straightened up and stepped back, folding his arms and smiling impishly at his friend. He glanced at Julie and saw Susie, their other lifelong friend, beside her. Julie and Susie stood quietly, wondering what Andrew was up to, and returned his impish look with questioning stares. Andrew just looked back and continued to smile. Julie waited to see what was about to play out. "So, Andrew, my friend," Matt continued, "what kind of gas engine is this?"

Andrew's smile grew in size as he cleared his throat. "The kind that delivers about two hundred thousand volts of electricity to the one holding it wrong if the switch is accidentally tripped."

Matt froze during a mid-air swipe. A look of pure terror flashed across his face as he gently replaced the device on the workbench and slowly backed away from the table. He looked around at the faces smiling at him. Julie and Susie tried hard to stifle their laughter. Matt cleared his throat.

"Well," Matt's voice was higher than he would have liked to hear, "that was fun. Uh, what are you doing with something like this, anyway?"

"It makes a great conversation piece," Andrew replied. Julie and Susie, no longer able to contain their laughter, sputtered out small chuckles at first and then full-blown laughter.

Matt's face turned a bright red at the embarrassment of being chided. "No, I'm serious," he said, "why would you need something that generates that much voltage?"

Andrew placed his hand on his friend's shoulder. "It takes a great deal of electricity to create the type of plasma I need to interact with the drive infusion unit. I need to create plasma to run my plasmatic engine. That's the type of fuel it will take. Plasma can be created in endless supplies and is clean."

Matt stared at Andrew with a blank expression. He opened his mouth, but nothing came out. After a moment, his mouth closed again as he thought better about what might escape.

"Do you understand?" Andrew asked.

Matt nodded his head up and down.

"So, you don't really understand then?"

"Not a word," Matt said, still nodding his affirmative response.

"Want a simpler explanation?"

"Uh, sure," Matt said.

"How about this," Andrew thought hard, then continued, "I need it for my experiments."

Matt threw his hands in the air. "Of course! Why didn't you say so in the first place?"

Susie, who had stopped laughing, stepped into the garage, leaving Julie's side. "Matt, leave him alone," she said. "What he's doing sounds really interesting."

Matt looked at his friend wide-eyed, "Are you telling me that you understand what he's saying?"

"Not entirely," Susie replied, "but from what I did understand, I think it's going to be cheaper than what we're paying at the pump." She looked at Andrew, "Is it for transportation use?"

"I'm not sure it can ever be used for cars," Andrew started, "but who knows? Maybe someday. But I have other plans in mind if, and I emphasize that word, if, I can ever even get it to work." Andrew's look went from exuberant to slightly downtrodden.

"You'll figure it out," Julie said, seeing his sudden mood change. "You just need to keep at it and give it time. You've already come up with some pretty cool ideas."

"You're wonderful," Andrew said, "but the truth is, my biggest discoveries are by accident. I don't think I know what I'm doing. It's just gut instinct at this point. Sometimes the things I create work, and sometimes they don't. I wish I had more formal training in this stuff."

"It doesn't matter how you find them," Matt said, clapping Andrew on the shoulder, "as long as you do. So, will you take a break with us and let all those ideas ruminate over a few beers with some friends tonight? I'll bet that Julie could use a night out." Matt glanced at Julie, proud of his attempt, but saw Julie barely shaking her head and giving Matt a stern look.

"We can go out anytime," Julie said to Andrew. "I've got a feeling about tonight."

"Good feeling or bad?" Susie asked.

"Not good or bad. Just a feeling, really," Julie said thoughtfully. "Something's going to happen. I don't know what, but something exciting, I'm sure."

Matt huffed. "Intuition. Why is it that you women always have it? The bad part is that it always seems to turn out right!" Matt turned to Andrew. "So I guess you're going to use this as an excuse to stay in and work, right buddy?" Matt chided.

"Can't argue with a woman's intuition, Matt," Andrew smiled.

Matt silently mimicked what Andrew had just said and shrugged his shoulders. "Fine. But don't come crying to me all boo hoo when you find yourself sitting in your house, all alone, with no place to go, and all of your friends are out enjoying themselves and having the time of their lives!"

"Yeah, yeah, whatever you say, big fella. Go home, Matt. Come back tomorrow, and we'll all go out."

Matt huffed. "I've heard that before." Then, smiling, Matt Said, "But if you make an earth-shattering discovery tonight, you'll need to tell us about it, and you're buying the beers!"

"You've got it, buddy!" Andrew said, smiling.

"Come on, Matt," Susie said, grabbing him by the collar. "Let's get going. We'll have plenty of time to visit tomorrow." She looked at Andrew, "Good luck tonight. See you tomorrow."

"Okay," Matt said. See you next time." Then Matt stood

tall—as tall as he could—and, in his best Terminator voice, proclaimed, "We'll be back!" He gave Andrew a handshake and a hug. Then Susie took her turn with the hug and goodbyes, and they walked into the house.

Julie started to walk in, then stopped and turned to Andrew. "Don't be too long. Dinner will be ready soon. Guess it's a good thing we didn't go out. We'd have to warm up tonight's dinner for leftovers."

"I won't be long," Andrew said, "and I love you."

Julie smiled understandingly and said, "I love you too." As she turned to go inside, the doorbell rang. Matt yelled, "Hey Julie, someone is at your door. Do you want me to get it on the way out?"

"Thanks, Matt," Julie yelled. "I'm coming right in."

Andrew watched Julie until she disappeared behind the closed kitchen door. "Andrew Barton," he said to himself, "you're a fortunate man!"

Julie entered the front room just as Susie and Matt reached the front door. Matt opened the door, and Dakota Martin, the Barton's babysitter, and her two friends, Alicia and Kylie, stood with backpacks and expectant looks. Matt mumbled a low "Hey" as he walked out, and Susie smiled.

Julie walked to the door. "Hi Kota! What's up?"

"Hi, Mrs. Barton," Kota said in her cheery voice. "I was doing some homework and, well, uh, I just don't get it."

Julie looked somewhat perplexed. "Don't your parents usually help you with your homework?"

"Yeah," Kota said, "but they're both working late tonight, and I have to get this assignment done by tomorrow. You see, the reason both Mom and Dad are working tonight is so we can all head down to Water World tomorrow. If I'm at Water World, I won't be able to finish my homework, so I've got to get it done tonight." Kota looked down. "They seem to be working late more and more recently, as well as weekends." She looked sad and far away but then snapped back and smiled at Julie. "Anyway, I was hoping that maybe you could help me with this part I'm stuck on." She turned and looked at her two friends. "I tried to ask my friends, but we can't agree on the answer to the last question."

Julie laughed, "And I thought they came along for moral support."

"Well, they came along to see who's right. I've looked everywhere in this stupid book and can't find the answer. I don't know why the teacher always makes us look up things that aren't in the book. It's frustrating. Anyway, we started arguing over who knew the subject the best."

The other two girls looked irritated. "Yeah, but Kylie knows I know this subject better," Alicia quipped.

"Better than what?" Kylie replied, ruffling.

Julie thought it best to jump in and moderate. "Maybe we should just look at the homework and then decide who's right about what." Julie motioned for them to come in and sit on the couch. The three girls plopped down like rag dolls tossed on the floor. Julie cringed, knowing their old couch was getting close to being a former old couch. *One more attack like that*, she thought, *and goodbye comfy couch, hello Goodwill.* Julie sat gingerly on the end cushion. "So," she started, "what is the homework about?"

Kota pulled a large, heavy book out of her backpack, lifting it up and smiling. "Plant science!" She sounded almost too pleased.

Julie, on the other hand, wasn't pleased at all. "Uh, plant science?" she said, sounding more doubtful than she wanted. "I really don't know anything about plant science except that you need to water and feed them. Even how much light they should get is a mystery to me sometimes."

The smile on Kota's face melted away, and she slowly lowered the book. "Oh," she said, sounding terribly disappointed. "I don't know what I'm going to do now." She started to put the book back in the backpack when Julie brightened up.

"Now, just because I don't know about plants doesn't mean all is lost," Julie said, smiling. "Mr. Barton has a degree in Agricultural Sciences, so he might know something about plants."

Kota's eyes widened, and her mouth dropped open so far that Julie thought it would entirely fall off her face. "Really?" she squealed, looking at her two friends. "That's awesome!" Then her expression changed to concern as she asked, "Uh, is Mr. B even around, though? Does he have time to help us?"

Julie reached over and took the heavy book from Kota. "He just happens to be in the garage working with his new experiment. He might need a break right about now. Let's go find out."

In the garage, Andrew was still sitting at his workbench and continued to tinker while speaking quietly to himself. He fiddled with some wires and said out loud, "This should do it." Andrew frequently spoke to himself out loud when no one was around. He wasn't sure why and was always embarrassed to find someone listening to him without his knowledge. Whatever the reason, he liked speaking out loud to work through problems. He'd answer himself as well, which helped resolve any outstanding issues.

He looked at the circuitry on the workbench. It was a lot —so many wires connected to so many circuits. He looked again and said to himself, "Okay, here we go. Hold on."

He closed his eyes and, cringing slightly, flipped the switch. He waited for something spectacular to happen. Nothing did. Nothing at all. Just the clicking sound of the switch. He slowly un-squinted his eyes, looked around the workbench, and immediately saw the problem. The loose wire on the back of the switch. He shook his head as if to show disgust at his lack of organization. It was too bad that he could never see himself shake his head. Perhaps he would have felt more shame if that were the case.

He turned off the switch and tightened the wire.

"This is it," he said. "Now, something is going to happen."

He closed his eyes again and flipped the switch.

CHAPTER 3

Hold On

When he heard the popping and crackling sound, his eyes flew open. The acrid smell of burning wires filled his nostrils. There was a human delay from when Andrew saw the sparks and smoke until he could turn off the switch. He grabbed one of his many fire extinguishers, put out the beginning of the small fire at the back of the workbench, and then returned the extinguisher to the floor. Frustrated, Andrew hit the top of the workbench with his fist and, in the process, didn't notice the magnetic ring slip, just slightly, down the plasma ball. He ran his fingers through his hair just as Julie and the girls opened the door from the kitchen to the garage and stepped out.

Andrew quickly reached over and pressed the button that opened the garage door. He stood up and started waving in the air to clear out the smoke lingering from the small fire. Seeing Andrew waving, Kota and her friends ran out to join him. The sight of the three teenage girls waving frantically in the air next to her husband made Julie start to laugh. Soon, they were all laughing, including Andrew! Slightly out of breath, he sat back down at his workbench.

"Oh goodness!" Andrew puffed. "It's great to be distracted sometimes. Thank you, girls, for picking this time to stop by. You made my mood soar to new heights! So, what brings you all to my humble workshop today?"

Julie caught her breath and said, "Kota needs some help with a problem, and I thought you would be the only person who could help her."

Andrew looked back and forth between Julie and Kota and smiled with the slightest hint of a sigh. "What can I do to help?" he asked.

"Well," Kota started, "it's about my plant science homework. Mrs. B said that you knew some stuff about plant science and that you might be able to help my friends and me decide the correct answer to this because they think one thing and I think something else, and we can't decide who is right."

Andrew always found it difficult to follow Kota when she spoke, as she tended to always speak quickly. For some reason, however, he could follow everything she was saying this time. "I used to love plant science when I was in college," he said. "So tell me what this problem is, and let's get to it."

Kota opened her book and walked to Andrew to show him the page. Kylie and Alicia stayed back but listened with interest as to what the correct answer might be.

Kota pointed to a passage on the page and said, "Well,

the problem involves mitochondria."

At first, Andrew felt a little unsure about what the question might entail, and he started to realize just how long it had been since his school days, but he took a breath and said, "Okay. What about them?"

"Well, the book really doesn't talk about their main purpose. It tells about how many there are and that they're organelles and stuff like that, but..."

Kota's friend, Kylie, interrupted, "But I said that they help the plants grow through replication."

Then Alicia had to have her turn, so she blurted out, "And I said it had something to do with the production of proteins. So, who's right?"

Andrew smiled to himself. He knew the answer to this and was pretty proud of himself. He said, "Well, their main function is the conversion of the potential energy of food molecules into ATP. Does that sound familiar to anything you've been taught in class?"

Kylie and Alicia looked at each other and then at Dakota. They smiled shyly and shrugged.

Kota looked up from the book. "Oh yeah. I remember that from class now. Thanks."

"No problem," Andrew said. "I'm glad I had the time to help."

"Yeah, me too," Kota said, putting her book back into

her backpack. "Seems like there's never enough time for things like friends or especially homework." She made a face at the word.

Andrew looked at his workbench and then at Julie and said, "It seems there is never enough time for the things we really want to do."

Andrew pushed the button on the wall that closed the garage door. As the door closed, Andrew noticed that Kylie was interested in what was on the workbench.

She saw that Andrew was looking at her and said, "Hey, Mr. B? What do you do out here anyway?" She continued to look, with intense curiosity, at the equipment on the workbench.

Andrew smiled at Kylie and knew she had the same curiosity he had at her age. "Well, I'm not sure I have enough time to completely answer that question, but let's just say I'm trying to invent some cool things."

Kota walked over to Kylie and started looking at everything as well. "There's so much stuff out here. Can we watch what you do someday? I mean, can we watch you work? It would be really cool to be one of the first people to actually see some great invention that you come up with that will change the world."

Andrew smiled and felt good being the center of attention. "We'll make time to do that someday if you really think you're interested. I'd love to show you what I'm working on, but I want to get further along with it before that happens. I'm sure that your parents wouldn't care much for you coming home with smoke inhalation."

"That would be very cool," Alicia said. "Thanks, Mr. B."

"You're welcome," Andrew said. "But right now, I need to get back to work."

Julie spread her arms and started gathering the girls like chickens in a farmyard. "C'mon, girls. Let's let Andrew finish what he's doing."

The girls each muttered their goodbyes and headed up the steps. Andrew smiled and waved and then sighed, turning back to the workbench.

Julie stopped at the top of the few steps leading from the garage into the kitchen and looked at Andrew. Andrew looked up at her and smiled back. She waited until the girls were just out of earshot and asked, "Are you sure you're okay?"

"Yeah, I'm fine," Andrew said. "Just a little discouraged with how things are going out here. You saw the smoke. Smoke bad. Smoke very bad."

"Try not to be too discouraged," Julie said encouragingly. "Just remember that you often can't immediately see the problem's solution. It hides, watching for the last thing you do and behind the last place you look. Just keep doing and then step back and keep looking."

"I'm so glad we're married," Andrew said. "Thank you, sweetheart."

"Aw shucks," Julie said jokingly. "It's nothing I wouldn't do for any of my other boyfriends." Julie winked at Andrew and smiled. "Don't be too long. Dinner is going to be ready really soon."

"I just want to try one more thing, then I'll be in," Andrew said, and his focus slowly shifted back toward the workbench and the mysteries that awaited him.

Julie smiled, shook her head, and walked in, closing the door behind her.

Andrew sighed and was slowly sucked back into his world of mystery. He looked back at his workbench and mentally went through each step that had led to the small fire. Each gadget and electronic item was meticulously inspected for something misplaced or loose. Once completed, Andrew slowly sat down. He replaced this component and that wire, checking and double-checking. Everything looked how it should, or at least the way he saw it in his mind.

"What am I doing wrong?" he asked himself and started pointing to the line of circuitry. He picked up a clipboard with a few pieces of paper on it and chuckled.

"Someday, I'm going to keep that promise I made myself and get more organized," he mumbled.

Andrew followed wires from one point to the next. He checked connections and then double-checked them again. One day, when he was at the university, going through the small warehouse that contained old science equipment to be sold to the public, he found a box of mysterious black boxes.

Each box had a red button on the end, a toggle switch on the top next to a small light, and four tiny screws on the bottom. He bought the entire box of boxes for ten dollars. He had no idea what the boxes did, nor did he understand the circuitry inside, but he used the black boxes as the main power switch for his current circuit. He took the box apart and poked at the various resistors, capacitors, and strange-looking things that he assumed were diodes. Everything seemed to be soldered well, so he put the bottom back on the box.

As he went over the circuit, he found a few loose connections but never noticed the faint glow from the plasma ball or the slightly shifted position of the magnetic ring. He sat in his chair and then stood up again. He was tired and wanted to sit down, but he thought it might be better to stand.

"Okay," he said to himself. "This is it. One more try."

The door into the house opened, and Julie stuck her head out. "Dinner's almost ready," she said. "Don't be much longer."

Andrew looked up at the digital clock just above his workbench, which displayed 7:05. He watched the colon blink a few times and realized that he was getting tired.

Andrew looked back at Julie. "I won't. I'm going to try one more thing, and then I should be in—fifteen minutes tops."

Julie smiled and slightly shook her head. "So I should plan on seeing you in about half an hour? I know how long your fifteen minutes can turn into."

Andrew smiled. "I know, but it will only be fifteen minutes this time. I promise."

Julie gave Andrew a look of half belief and half pity and then turned back inside.

Andrew checked a few more circuits and connections with the setup on the workbench. He felt like he couldn't check them enough. Perhaps he was just putting off activating it and not wanting to flip that switch, only to face what could be another failure. Whatever it was, he finally convinced himself to try. "Andrew," he said out loud, "if you continue to sit and do nothing, then nothing will be the end result." He took a deep breath and made the big decision. It was time to try again. He put on his safety goggles, cringed slightly, and flipped a switch. As before, nothing happened.

Confused and frustrated, Andrew looked at the mess in front of him. "I just checked everything. What could it be?"

He looked at the connections again and realized that he had not hooked the black box back up. "I guess it helps when the main switch is actually in the line."

He hooked up the black box and looked up at the clock again. It now read 7:10. Reflexively, he cringed slightly as he flipped the switch hoping for a different result than the last time.

CHAPTER 4

Changes

There was an explosion. Andrew didn't know how big it was or how long it lasted because, as he recalled, things flew everywhere. Still, then, as he remembered, it looked like the debris froze in the air and was suddenly sucked back to its original position.

Regardless of what he thought he saw earlier, Andrew realized his eyes were closed, and he was lying on a hard, cold surface. Andrew opened his eyes. He was lying on the garage floor.

It was difficult, but Andrew sat up unsteadily and removed his goggles. He was frustrated and looked down at the ground. Looking back up at his workbench, Andrew stared at the clock. It now read 7:05. How did he get on this side of the garage? The door to the house opened, and Julie walked out in her bathrobe, heading toward the refrigerator in the garage. She looked over and saw Andrew sitting on the ground, looking very confused.

"Andrew! Holy cow. You scared the crap out of me. I thought I just left you upstairs in bed, asleep. How did you get dressed and down here so fast? And how did you get so dirty already?"

"I," Andrew didn't know what to say, "I've been down here for a while."

Julie laughed and shook her head. "You just can't wait to get at your experiments, can you? Well, go ahead and work, and I'll have breakfast ready in a little while. Then you can come in and take a shower before you come back out. And try not to get too dirty again."

"Yeah. I promise. I just need to look over a few things," Andrew said, standing. "I want to see if I have this circuit hooked up correctly. Something happened. I'm not certain what, but something strange. I guess you were right."

"I was right?" Julie asked. "Well, that's a different statement. You never say that! What was I right about, Andrew?"

"Earlier, when you said you had a feeling about tonight," Andrew replied.

"Tonight?" Julie asked.

Julie walked across the garage, grabbed the eggs from the refrigerator, and turned to go back inside. She stopped, turned, and looked at Andrew.

"Your intuition, remember?"

"Andrew, I don't know what you're talking about. You were sleeping when I left the bedroom, and now you're here. We didn't talk about anything. Are you feeling okay, Andrew? Do you think maybe you dreamed this whole event?"

"Julie?" Andrew said, stopping her.

"What is it, sweetheart?"

"This may sound strange, but what day is it?"

Julie looked at Andrew, concerned, and said, "It's Saturday. All day. How could you forget? You were looking forward to today all week."

"Just had one of those moments," he said, smiling. "I just wanted to make sure I was thinking correctly. Thanks, hon. I'll be in shortly. Love you."

"Love you too," she said, looking at him suspiciously and walking into the house.

Andrew wondered if he was slowly going crazy until he walked to the workbench and picked up his clipboard. He stared at the writing on the top sheet of paper. He read the notes he had written early Saturday evening or at least the note he would write later today. It took him a while to understand what had happened. He went back in time twelve hours. Something else was wrong, though. He didn't know what, but Julie didn't seem like herself. He needed to figure out the totality of what happened.

He walked into the house and gave Julie a hug. She pushed him away. "Andrew, you're filthy and smell like burning wires. The stairs are right there. Use them to go to the shower and clean up. Then, and only then, may you hug me."

After his shower, Andrew walked to the kitchen table and sat down.

Julie brought a plate of food and set it in front of Andrew. She sniffed at him. "Much better," she said, wrapping her arms around his neck and squeezing him tight.

"I'm glad you approve," Andrew said, taking a bite of food.

After breakfast, Andrew went back out to the garage.
He needed to figure out what he had done that created this
situation, threw him back in time, and dramatically changed
things. He had much to think about.

He wondered where his other self was, the self that
was here earlier.

He knew what would happen today since he had been
thrown back in time. He had lived it before. At least, he
thought he had until his two girls came bounding out from
the kitchen. He didn't know what to think. He didn't know his
own children. Stephanie looked younger. He learned his other
daughter was named Joanna.

Andrew needed to learn more about his own life!

Going back into the house, Andrew found Julie.

"Well, this is different," Julie said to Andrew. "What's
up with you today? You seem a little different. A little off."

"I slept badly last night," he said. "Can we do
something a little different today?" Andrew asked.

"What did you have in mind?"

"Can we look through our memory boxes?"

Julie looked at Andrew. "What?" She said. "Why?"

"We haven't looked at them in a while, and I feel
nostalgic. Do you mind?"

"Um, okay," she said and headed toward the stairs.
Andrew followed.

They spent most of the rest of the morning looking
through memory boxes, and Andrew tried to figure out who
he was and what he had done.

"Do you remember when we first fell in love?"
Andrew asked.

"Of course I do, silly," she said, affectionately pushing

him on the shoulder. "We went out to Pan's Pizza with my friend and your friends. Something clicked, and it was love at fifth sight."

Andrew remembered things much differently but said nothing, only nodding and smiling.

Eventually, he made his way back out to the garage. He could undo what he had done.

"Andrew," Julie called through the door from the kitchen to the garage.

"Yeah." Andrew's reply was automated and not conscious.

"Andrew. Matt and Susie are here."

"Uh huh," Andrew replied again, not hearing the statement.

Andrew learned a few things about his relationship with Julie in this timeline. They had been married for eight years. They dated in college, where they both attended, and married shortly after graduation. They had their ups and downs and struggled to make a good life and a wonderful home filled with love, desire, friendship, and the occasional romp in the hay. It was because of the latter that they had two children. Stephanie, five years old, and Joanna, three years old. Stephanie looked the same as he remembered her at five years old, but yesterday, in his mind, she was eight. Somehow, he had changed the timeline. Okay, for those who had lived this timeline, but it was confusing for Andrew, whose memories and past life reflected something that neither he nor anyone else in this time would remember!

Between these thoughts and trying to figure out what he had done to create this rift, he wasn't hearing his wife. He was lost in the pursuit of correcting what he had done.

"Andrew!" Julie yelled to get his attention. Andrew felt like a stranger and didn't know this Julie at all. She was the same but somehow different.

"Andrew, are you hearing me?"

"Sure, honey. I'll be right there."

She threw a damp dishtowel at him.

"Whoa, whoa, whoa!" he exclaimed. "I'm working with high-voltage equipment here. You don't want bar-b-qued Andrew in the garage now, do you?"

"If he would pay attention to his wife yelling his name, yes! Andrew," Julie huffed. "I've been trying to get your attention repeatedly."

"Well, you should have come out here instead of standing inside hollering for me." Andrew threw the dishtowel over his shoulder.

"She was standing here the entire time, buddy." Matt Berman squeezed his way past Julie with a muffled "Sorry. Excuse me" and a silly smile. Andrew and Matt had been friends since high school. They met Julie in college. The typical small-town group that stayed while the town grew up around them. Matt had been the State Champ on the wrestling team. He loved chess and was quite intelligent, although Andrew sometimes wondered if Matt hid that intelligence in the back room of his brain. He preferred to have fun than to be serious in life. "You really should pay more attention to this lovely young girl. Don't know why she sticks around you anyway." Matt grinned from ear to ear. He had always teased Andrew and probably would until their final days.

"If she left me, she'd have to go to you, and she's not interested in trading down," Andrew replied.

"Good one, buddy!" Matt said, walking over and giving Andrew a hug.

Matt hugged Andrew, and another friend, Susie Montgomery, walked into the kitchen doorway and put her hands on Julie's shoulders. "Aw, Julie," Susie said in a mock sentimental tone, "looks like the boys finally found each other. Guess that means you and I will have to take the kids and run away."

"Dork!" Julie laughed and gave Susie a hug.

"Well, well," Matt said, "looks like we're getting our own little orgy going on." He raised his eyebrows up and down.

"Only in your dreams, Matthew," Susie said, "and please keep those dreams private. We all haven't eaten yet, and I don't want to ruin my appetite.

"Oh, Susie," Matt continued mockingly, "you've wanted me since high school, and you know it's true. It's just our friendship that has stood in the way of true romance!"

Susie turned sideways, bent over, and put her finger in her mouth, presenting the group with a fake gagging scene. She and Matt had continued with this type of relationship for years. Neither was married. Both enjoyed a carefree single lifestyle. But an outside onlooker would swear that something was going on between the two of them. If there was, however, they hid it very well from the rest of the world.

"Well," Andrew said, "I hate to break up this little gathering of memory memorabilia, but I need to get back to work." Andrew turned back toward the workbench, looked up as no one moved, and stared at him. "What?"

Julie walked over to Andrew and removed the dishtowel from his shoulder. At first, she thought about rolling it up and snapping him with it, but then she thought maybe she'd save that for later. "Matt and Susie came over today because we, you and I, promised them that we would go out with them."

"We did?"

"Yes."

"When...uh, when did we do this?" Andrew was talking in a whisper.

"Last weekend," Julie said. "Remember when you said you had to work last weekend but promised that we could all go out this weekend?" Julie wanted to go out. It had been too long, and she didn't feel like letting Andrew ruin the expected afternoon for her.

"I...I said that?" Andrew started doing his Nicholas Cage imitation, although he looked nothing like him. "Let me see. Are you sure I said that because I really, really have no recollection of saying anything like that?" He looked at Matt, "Do you remember me saying anything like that, Matthew?"

"Yes, I do, and it's Matt, not Matthew. Sounds so stuffy. Now, come on, and let's go. Don't make me hit you with this…" Matt picked up a long rod with a wire trailing from it that looked like an antenna. He started waving it around like a sword.

"Matt, you might want to put that down," Andrew said, pulling Julie behind him.

"And why is that, my good man? Afraid I'll thrash you?" Matt was on a roll.

"No," Andrew answered calmly, "but I am afraid that you'll hurt yourself or someone around you if that wire happens to connect and the two hundred thousand volts of electricity it carries reaches you."

Matt froze in mid-air. He looked at his hand, holding the long metal wand. He slowly put the wand back down on the workbench where it originally lay, looking up and laughing nervously. "You, uh, weren't serious, though, right? Just joking?"

"Nope," Andrew said as he reached over and flipped the switch on a black box to 'off.'

"What the hell are you doing playing with stuff like this?"

"Not playing. It's part of my experiments."

"Making a replacement for the electric chair?" Matt was a little miffed. "And why would you leave it lying around, all charged up, for someone to reach out and electrocute themselves?"

"I didn't know you were coming over," Andrew grumbled.

"Yes, you did!" Matt insisted.

"You did, Andrew," Susie said.

Andrew looked at Julie. She nodded.

"I don't remember any of this." He thought hard about the situation. "Okay, let me ask you this!"

"Ask me what?" Julie sighed.

"If we were supposed to go out, then what about the girls?"

"I'm assuming you mean our little girls?" Julie teased.

"Of course, that's who I mean," Andrew replied. "Who else would I mean? If we were going out, we would have found someone to babysit."

"Hey, Mr. B," Kota, the 18-year-old girl from down the street, appeared behind Susie. "I'm here to babysit. Sorry, I'm a little late."

Andrew stared at Kota. He felt everyone's eyes on him, and he didn't want to look back until the blood started draining from his face.

"Hi Kota," he stammered. "Hey, no problem. We were just talking about where we wanted to go, so, uh, you came at just the right time." Then he glanced at everyone, "Okay folks, let's not just stand around, let's get going. I want to get back early to get back on this experiment." With that, he rushed through the kitchen door. Everyone else stood dumbstruck and, after shaking their heads, followed Andrew through the house.

Julie caught up with him ahead of the others. "Andrew, what is wrong with you?"

"This isn't how the day was supposed to happen. It's not how I remember it happening."

"What are you talking about?" Julie said.

"I've lived this day before, but it's suddenly going differently." He turned to Julie. "I was working on my experiment for the plasmatic drive. It was Saturday. Today. Well, tonight. I flipped the switch, and the next thing I knew, I was on the garage floor, and it was this morning. That's why you thought you left me in the bedroom, and I was suddenly in the garage, all dirty."

Julie looked at Andrew suspiciously. "Uh-huh," she said. "You've already lived this day? Did it include some early rum and cokes without me?"

Matt and Susie walked up. "Déjà vu, eh Andrew?"

"What? No, not at all. No Déjà about it."

Julie pulled Andrew by the sleeve and looked at Matt. "Would you excuse us for just a moment?"

"Whatever," Matt said. "It's not like we have to be

there at a certain time. We have all night!"

Julie pulled Andrew up the stairs and into their bedroom. She shut the door and turned to look at Andrew. "What is going on with you?"

"Let me try to explain this again," Andrew said, increasingly frustrated. "I know this is hard to believe, but do you remember this morning when you found me in the garage, and you thought I was still upstairs?"

"Oh, here we go again," Julie said. "Yes, I remember this day very well. Much better than you do, it would seem."

"Okay. Yeah. Well, I was sitting there because I had been thrown back in time from an experiment I successfully did at seven o'clock tonight." Andrew realized how crazy the words sounded after he finished the sentence.

Julie was speechless at first but then said, "Andrew, we are going out. I haven't been out in a really long time, and you promised that we would do this with our friends today, so get your butt downstairs and don't ruin the day."

At this point, he realized that not only had he changed the timeline of events, but he also had somehow changed his wife. He smiled at her and kissed her. "Let's go have some fun!" he said, trotting down the stairs. Julie just stared, narrowed her eyes, and followed Andrew out of the room.

CHAPTER 5

Time Change

They had a great afternoon at the sports bar, devouring hot wings and fries, downing large quantities of beverages, and laughing until their sides hurt.

When Andrew and Julie returned home, Andrew headed straight to the garage. Julie followed and stood at the kitchen door. "Sometimes I wonder who married you. Me, or this garage."

Andrew laughed. "I was just on a roll when Matt and Susie stopped by, and I didn't want to lose my train of thought. This could be big!"

Silly man, Julie thought. "Okay. But don't be long, please. I'd like to get a little of you tonight, too."

"I promise," Andrew said. He looked at the clock. "Tell you what. It's 5:00 now, so what if I work out here until 7? Then, when I come in, the rest of the night belongs to you. Deal?"

"Deal," Julie said, and walked out, kissed him firmly on the lips, and walked back to the kitchen. Before closing the door, she looked at Andrew and said, "7 o'clock. I'll come out and remind you."

"You won't have to remind me. I'll keep track of the time."

Julie just smiled, shaking her head slightly, and closed the door.

Andrew continued working. Hooking up wires, increasing and decreasing voltages. At some point, a small explosion popped and was followed by a small fire. He raced feverishly to put it out, fearing that the sound of the explosion would summon his wife to the garage, to be followed by a series of screams and panicky gestures, but she never appeared. He continued working and lost track of time. He was about to hook up a circuit he remembered from the previous time he did this and knew it would do something when the door opened, and Julie stuck her head out. "It's just about 7:05, Andrew."

Andrew looked up with the eyes of a puppy, hoping for a treat. "Ten more minutes?" he asked.

"I know how your 'ten more minutes' are, so I'll give you twenty, but no more. Dinner will be ready at 7:30, and I've made shrimp. I don't want it to overcook." Julie said sternly.

Andrew smiled. "Thanks, sweetheart!" he said and quickly returned to work.

Julie closed the door.

Andrew double-checked to see if everything was hooked up. He mentally crossed his fingers and threw the switch on the black box. Nothing. Only the click of the switch. *What happened?* he thought. *I did everything right.* He started at the point of the emitter and traced backward. He checked every circuit, every connection, and every wire. He kept tracing back through the black box to the...unplugged cord. *Gaaaaa! How stupid can I get? Double-check the circuits but forget to give it power.* Andrew shook his head and smiled at his stupidity. He looked up at the clock. 7:25 he thought. *Last try.* He plugged in the cord and turned to the black box. The switch was in the 'on' position. He looked up at the emitter and saw a deep purple glow and a low hum. He looked closer at the emitter tip and saw the glow pulsing. Suddenly, the glow grew incredibly bright. Andrew felt as if an entire football team defensive line plowed into him. He felt objects hit his back. No, apparently he was flying across the room and his back was running into things. The humming stopped. It was dark. Wait, maybe it wasn't. He opened his eyes. Still light in here, he thought. He looked around, expecting to see a mess from the explosion. No mess. In fact, nothing was disturbed at all, but there was movement. Nothing solid, just a faint shadow at his workbench. He looked hard, trying to make out the shape. While he was looking in that direction, he noticed the clock. *7:05?* He thought. *How can it be? Morning again, or evening? Am I in the same timeline, or did I totally mess this up this time...?* The kitchen door opening interrupted his thoughts. It was Julie. She poked her head out and spoke, "It's just about 7:05, Andrew." She looked at the workbench, confused, and then around the garage until her eyes landed on Andrew, still sitting on the floor. "Taking a rest?"

Andrew looked over at the workbench. He recognized the shadow as him, where he was, and what he was doing a few minutes earlier. The image vanished. "Are you okay?"

Julie asked.

"Yeah," Andrew stammered. "Yeah, I think so. But you already came out and told me it was 7:05."

"Of course," Julie said. "Just now because it's 7:05."

"No, you came out earlier and told me. Then you said I could have 20 more minutes," Andrew said as he got up.

"Well, if you need it, I could let you stay out here for another 20 minutes, but you should come inside if you're tired of working," Julie said, a little worried about him.

"Shrimp!" Andrew exclaimed and ran over to his workbench.

"What?" Julie exclaimed.

"You told me I had to be in by 7:30 because you were making shrimp, and you didn't want it overcooked," Andrew said.

"Um, not really, I'm making a roast, but shrimp sounds really good. Maybe I can make that tomorrow night for dinner. What do you think?."

"No," Andrew said, "You told me when you came out the first time that you were making shrimp."

"Andrew, sweetheart," Julie said softly, "this is the first time I have come out here since five o'clock. Did you fall asleep?"

"No, I was working on this emitter and checking the circuits." He looked over at the plug, which was out of the socket. "This plug was out, and when I plugged it back in, there was a flash, and I must have been knocked back in time a few minutes. Yeah, it was 7:25 when I did it."

Julie looked very concerned now. "Why not just come in and sit down, Andrew."

"I know it happened," he said, plugging the plug back

into the outlet. Nothing happened. *Wait,* he thought, *I turned the black box switch on while checking the circuits. I haven't done that yet.* He reached over and flipped the switch to on. The emitter began to glow with the same bright flash. He was on the ground again. He looked at the clock. 7:05. He saw this time, two images at his workbench and the image of Julie at the door. *Echoes in time,* he thought. He stood up and ran to the door, and waited. The door opened and Julie was face to face with Andrew.

"Oh!" she started. "You scared the crap out of me!"

"Sorry," Andrew said, smiling. "I know you came out to tell me it's 7:05, that I can have 20 more minutes if I want and no more, and that we're having shrimp tonight."

"This is a lot of Deja vu," Julie said. "It's like we've done this a little differently before. Only thing is, we're not having shrimp. I made fajitas."

"But I thought you were making shrimp because we went out with Matt and Susie earlier, and you were still feeling full."

"We never went out with Matt and Susie today. Are you okay? Susie wasn't feeling well, so they canceled. Don't you remember? I came out and told you earlier." Julie put her hand on Andrew's forehead.

"I'm not sick," Andrew said.

"Then what are you talking about?" Julie asked.

"I'm coming in now," Andrew said excitedly. "I have a lot to tell you. I've already changed history twice; this time, I'm about to change our future! I love you!" He grabbed Julie and gave her a big kiss.

"I'm not sure how you changed history," she smiled, "but I can see what our future has in store tonight!" She grinned.

"That will be fun, but I must tell you this over dinner!"

They started to go inside when Andrew stopped. "Let me make a quick note."

Julie gave him a stern look.

"No, really," he said. "You can even leave the door open. I just want to write something down, so I don't forget."

"One thing, Andrew Barton. Write down one thing, then get inside!" Julie placed a hand on her hip and waggled her finger at him, and then she smiled and winked before turning to walk inside.

Andrew walked over to the clipboard and picked it up. He wrote:

I'm not sure what happened. Either I'm going crazy, or I just became the first person to travel back in time. It wasn't a giant leap back, just five minutes, but I can't dispute it. The clock went back five minutes, and certain events repeated themselves. Not all events, just a few. Makes me wonder how set the timeline really is. It makes me speculate that there are variations in the timeline. If so, where do the other time streams flow to? I guess I'll find out tomorrow when I continue working.

Andrew put the clipboard down and calmly walked into the house, where he found Julie setting dishes on the table. She looked up when she heard the door closing and smiled at Andrew.

"You didn't have to rush right in," she said. "I figured I wouldn't see you for a while."

"At least 20 minutes?" he said smiling.

Julie stopped what she was doing and looked at

Andrew suspiciously. "How did you know that? Learning mind reading now, are you?"

"No, but I do have a few things I need to tell you about. Something wonderful just happened."

"Okay," Julie said, putting the silverware on the table, "but hold on a second. Why don't you wash up first? We can talk about it over dinner. You're a real mess."

Andrew looked down at his hands and realized they were smudged with smoke soot. He nodded to Julie and walked into the bathroom to clean up a little.

When he returned to the kitchen, the table had been set, and dinner was waiting. Fajitas sizzled on the table pan and smelled delicious.

"I didn't know you knew how to make fajitas," Andrew said.

Julie laughed. "Goof. They're your favorite. We have them so often that sometimes I get tired of making them."

Andrew looked at his smiling wife. She was Julie, but not Julie. He wondered, now, what he might have done by messing with time and if he would ever get back to the Julie, he married.

"So, what's all this exciting news you want to tell me about?" Julie said while placing the meat and veggies on her tortilla.

"The most amazing thing happened," Andrew started. "I'm not sure what I did exactly or how I did it, but just a little bit ago, I was able to…"

The doorbell ringing interrupted Andrew.

"I'll get it. Just hold that thought. It sounds exciting, and I can't wait to hear about it." Julie got up from the table and trotted off to answer the front door.

When Julie opened the door, she was surprised to see Kota standing on the porch. "Hi, Mrs. Barton. Sorry to bother you again, but I forgot my book."

Julie smiled and opened the door wider, inviting Kota inside. "It's not a bother. We were just getting ready to sit down for dinner. Have you eaten?"

Kota smiled. "No. Not yet, but my mom came home early and is making dinner right now, so I need to get back."

"That's good," Julie said. "Well, come in, and we'll find your book."

Kota entered the house and walked into the living room. She looked around the front room and saw her book sitting on the coffee table. "Oh, duh! Here it is; I must have set it down without thinking, and it was right before me when I looked. Good thing it wasn't a tiger!"

The two girls laughed as Andrew walked into the living room.

"Hey, where did you go? I still have a lot to tell you," Andrew said and then saw that Kota was also in the room. "Oh, hi, Kota. What brings you here?"

Kota picked up her book. "I forgot my book. But I should get going. I told my mom I wouldn't be long."

"Wait. Your book?" Andrew said. "I could swear that I saw you put your book into your backpack in the garage."

Kota thought. "No, I don't think so. I'm pretty sure I came back inside and put it down just before Mrs. B got me a drink of water."

"But I'm sure tha…"

"Andrew! She needs to get home. And besides, we'll see her Friday night to watch Stephanie."

"I'll be here!" Kota said enthusiastically.

"That's great," Julie said, starting to walk Kota to the door. Kota stopped and turned toward Andrew.

"Mr. Barton?" she said.

"Yes, Kota?" Andrew replied.

"You know how we talked earlier about there never being enough time for things you enjoy and how precious time is?"

"Yes," Andrew said.

"Well, I was thinking about that and had a theory. Since it's the enjoyable things that make time fly by, time might slow down if no one enjoys themselves. What do you think?"

"Maybe," Andrew smiled. "Interesting theory. But I suspect it would only apply to one person at a time."

"Yeah. So then I thought if time slowed down for everyone, then it would seem normal. So, never mind. We probably can't do anything about time anyway."

"Time is a strange thing," Andrew said, thinking about what had happened throughout the day. "We always have theories about it. We dream of controlling it, but it always seems outside our reach. I have a theory, though, about..."

Julie touched Andrew's arm. "We need to let her get home, and we need to eat dinner. Maybe you two can discuss your theories another time."

"Yeah," Andrew said. "Another time."

After letting Kota out, Julie and Andrew returned to the table, where Andrew excitedly told Julie about his day. She listened patiently, nodded in the correct places, and silently wondered if her husband had lost his mind. However, she would wait a few days to make that decision.

During their conversation, something else was happening without their knowledge. In the darkness of the empty garage, on the workbench, the emitter sparked slightly. A voice could barely be heard coming from nowhere—almost a whisper—a deep and low whisper that had a sinister feel. The voice was there, but not there—in the same place and yet somewhere far away.

"Did you feel that?" The voice said.

A second voice answered, "I could not only feel it, but it was strong enough of a time displacement to register on the magnetograph."

"I must know what it was and where it came from," replied the first voice. "Track its origin. Find it, or your life will end."

"I live only to serve…"

CHAPTER 6

To Float or Not to Float

When I was a young boy, I loved magic. I always tried to figure out how these magical moments of deception happened. That's when I learned that sometimes what you see might not accurately represent what is actually there. While we grow up learning to believe what we see, we soon learn that, occasionally, deceptions are happening in front of our very noses! Table magic can make us scratch our heads. Street magic can make us believe in things that defy real life. I have dreamed about different realities and tried to make them appear. One day, I was looking for something no one had seen before. Something completely different. I found it and realized it wasn't what I needed after all. ~ *Andrew Barton*

"What a week it's been," Andrew said to Julie. "It seemed to plod along and go by so slowly."

"Well," Julie said, looking through the television channels, "it's Friday night, and you can put all that behind you now. Tomorrow, you can spend time in the garage working on your projects. I can't wait to see what you discover next. My only hope is that we can use it to make a little more money."

"I could always make a printing press and print our own," Andrew joked.

"Not funny," Julie said without looking at Andrew.

Andrew thought about the past week in detail. Although he noticed a few things slightly different than he thought they should be, he wasn't sure if it was because of his experiments or overactive imagination. People seemed to be the same for the most part. All the trees on the way to his work were accounted for. But something still felt off. It could be his imagination. He knew that his Julie never made fajitas and she never sat in front of the TV this much. Andrew wasn't a big fan of fajitas or TV, so he surmised that his counterpart in this timeline enjoyed those things. There were other things. Minor differences that were almost too slight to identify. Like leaving on a trip and having that nagging feeling you've forgotten something but can't figure out what it is.

Sometimes, it turns out to be nothing, but other times, it can be one of the most important things ever! The biggest thing that worried Andrew was, if he was here, where had this dimension's Andrew gone? You hear stories about people who apparently changed overnight into someone that their family didn't seem to know anymore. Could it be that others had experimented with the inter-dimensional shifts Andrew had? Had these people changed places with their counterparts? He had no idea but was afraid to think about it further, fearing that he might discover the answer. And yet, the thought of what his family might be noticing about his counterpart concerned him. That's the final thought he had before drifting off to sleep.

Andrew opened his eyes and stretched. He felt Julie stir next to him. "Good morning, sweetheart," he said. "Happy Saturday!"

Julie mumbled something unintelligible, turned over, and almost immediately started snoring.

"It's Saturday," he whispered, "and time for me to head down to tinker and experiment."

Andrew chose to experiment with a portion of the time thing for a while and then focused on something else. He had the opportunity to try one or two things during the week, much to the dismay of Julie. But once Andrew showed her what he was doing, even she had to admit it was impressive. So Andrew was sure she wouldn't be too upset with him running to the university warehouse to pick up more gadgets. He left the house and didn't notice there was something out of the ordinary just down the street.

Inside the van, two men sat wearing sunglasses, one in a suit and the other dressed casually. The driver watched Andrew's house intently. As Andrew entered the house, the driver picked up a tablet and typed some notes. He glanced up again and then put the tablet down. He stared again at the house and shook his head. He picked up the microphone on the two-way radio and spoke. "Surveillance 1, the subject has returned. Should we maintain surveillance?"

A voice crackled out of the speaker, speaking with no emotion. "Affirmative. Keep him under surveillance. We need to know more about his projects before we move in." The driver lowered the microphone and smiled slightly. He enjoyed his work. He loved taking down nut cases that were hell-bent on destroying the government. He was sure that this person, Andrew Barton, was one of those people. A nut case, a rebel, and a threat to not only this great nation but, quite possibly, the world! He picked up the tablet, navigated to his subject folder, and opened it.

He started reading through it again. He enjoyed learning about his prey over and over. Works in a warehouse. Has a degree in Agricultural Sciences. Married with one child. In debt. "He's in this for the money," he said out loud.

"What?" His partner in the passenger's seat looked up from his cell phone, which he was using to check his Facebook page.

"If you would spend less time staring at your phone and playing silly games, you might get somewhere important in this organization."

"I'm sitting in a car with you, watching some poor guy that really doesn't stand a chance with any little experiments he's doing, thanks to us. He's broke, yeah. So, he probably isn't even doing anything noteworthy. Just because one person complained and it landed in our laps doesn't mean that he's going to change the world with his penny ante experiments. The point being that you're always acting like a big shot, and we're still doing the same thing! Sitting in a car, in the heat of the day, in suits no less, watching some poor guy's house and hoping that someday we'll get an office job or maybe investigate some real crime."

"Shut up and watch how I work," the driver said. "Maybe you'll learn something!" The driver turned his attention back to the house to watch for any strange activity.

Andrew carried the box with his odd assortment of devices into the house. Julie was sitting on the couch, reading. She looked up as the door opened and smiled as Andrew awkwardly walked in. "Hi, hon." Did you find anything good today?"

"Yeah," Andrew replied, putting the large box on the floor. "I'll be able to use this in my POD." Andrew grinned from ear to ear.

"POD?" Julie questioned?

"You remember. I'm sure I told you about the POD I'm building. It stands for Personal Orientational Device. I hope it will take the rider to any location they want to visit." Andrew replied, sitting next to her on the couch.

"No, you never tell me anything you remember telling me," Julie said jokingly. Then, more seriously, "I'm pretty sure I'd remember you telling me something about a POD. But just in case I missed it, remind me, please."

"I'm sure I told you. It was the other night, or, no, wait, I remember, it was...no, but anyway, I'm sure I told you," Andrew was flustered, and his face flushed.

"Okay. If you say so. Why not humor me, though, and tell me again, what's this POD you're building?" Julie knew that Andrew had a tendency to not remember things he didn't tell her.

"Well, remember when I told you about the kickback into time I had?" Andrew asked.

"The 5 minutes?" She remembered the conversation. Julie needed to hear more about the time story but, at the same time, was tired of hearing about it. She hoped that this 'POD' would take them on a different path.

"Yeah. Well, I've been working on trying to control whether it's forward or backward, and I've been experimenting on a larger scale."

"Okay," Julie was being cautious. She wanted to know what he was talking about but didn't want him to take off into a rambling explanation she couldn't follow. *Funny,* Julie thought, *how well you get to know someone after living with them for so many years.* Yet she knew that ten years was not that long. "So the POD is a time machine?"

"Yeah, well, sort of," Andrew said. "The POD will allow me to control time travel but can also be used as a travel device while staying in the present, and maybe I can even take two or three people with me." Andrew waited for her reply.

"Like a vacation for you and me to anywhere in time?" Julie hoped but knew what the answer would be.

"No. I mean, I didn't think you were interested in going on time journeys." Andrew didn't even think about putting the love of his life in harm's way. He never really thought it would harm him, but he wasn't sure.

"I understand," she said, taking his hand. "Maybe not until you've perfected it. Someone's got to be here with Stephanie." She smiled at him. He wasn't sure if it was a smile of understanding or if she was humoring him.

Andrew asked her in a sentimental tone, "Are you worried about me?"

"Sometimes," she replied. "But I figure you won't do anything that will take you away from us."

"Not intentionally," he said, realizing his words were poorly chosen.

Julie shot him a look, then said, "Better not be at all." She was beginning to get angry at his line of thought.

Andrew moved closer to Julie. "I love you and Stephanie. You know I'd never do anything to hurt our family."

"I know. But I still have to worry sometimes." Julie looked up at Andrew and smiled. "Why don't you go to the garage and install that into your POD? Experiment with it carefully, and then we can talk more about it, okay?"

"Thanks, sweetheart," he replied with a big grin. "I won't be out there very long."

"Whatever. Just take the time you need." Julie loved him more than anything and would do anything to keep them together. She believed that he believed in what he was doing, but she always thought that, in her heart, the things he was saying were just hopeful prophecies. She hoped so anyway.

"I'll be in soon," he said, kissing her with the same kiss he gave her when they first met. The same kiss. They would never get tired of each other. They would never be parted. He knew that with all of his heart, but his mind wondered.

"Okay," she said. She also knew they would always be together and loved him beyond anything imaginable.

Andrew started to get up from the couch and picked up the box he had set on the floor, with the large coil sticking out.

"Hey, Andrew?" Julie called out.

"Yeah?"

"How much did that little device cost?" She knew that sometimes he didn't worry about the monthly household bills and where the money needed to go. Andrew was blinded by his love for his experiments. He couldn't see the household's financial well-being as it was affected by his spending.

"Well, um, it wasn't too much," Andrew replied. His face became a little too red for Julie's comfort.

"How much isn't too much?" Julie folded her arms, and her face took on a scolding look.

"Less than a hundred dollars," Andrew replied, trying to avoid the answer.

"How much less?" she demanded.

"Would you believe $20?" he asked, hoping to curb any further questioning.

Julie would not be put off. "Not really," she said, waiting for the proper answer.

"How about $21?"

Julie sighed in exasperation. Andrew knew he was fighting a losing battle.

"Go out and work," she said, knowing she wouldn't get the answer she wanted anytime soon. She would just have to look at the checking account online later.

"Thanks, sweetheart," he said, relieved. "And hey?"

"What?" Julie asked.

"Would you mind coming out in a few minutes and bringing the video camera?"

"Sure, what for?" She already knew the answer, but she hoped it would be different this time. She had videoed so many failures that she wanted to video one, just one success. It would mean so much to him and maybe help her have a little more faith in what he was doing.

"I'm going to try out this new magnetic flux oscillator I've been working on. If it works how I hope it will, I should be able to float in the air," Andrew said.

"The way you've been floating all sorts of little things around the house and scaring the devil out of me?"

"Sorry, hun. I didn't mean to. I've just been so excited about this new development," he said, slightly embarrassed again.

Julie shook her head. "You and your toys. I'll be there in a bit. Just promise you'll warn me before you do anything unexpected. Can you do that? I'd hate to drop the camera. It's the only one we have, and we can't afford a new one."

Andrew smiled, picked up his new toy, and headed to the garage. Julie shook her head and put down her book. She wondered what this would all mean and how it would change their lives if what Andrew was doing actually worked. He's brilliant but has tried so many things without success. What if, this time, it actually worked? She wondered at the possibilities. She hoped for success. She worried about their well-being financially. She wondered how he ever got so involved in this crazy life he developed, and then she sighed.

Andrew walked out into the garage and put his device down. He walked over to his workbench, picked up a black box, and smiled as his thoughts drifted elsewhere. Andrew put on a harness and adjusted a few knobs. As he ensured that the harness fit just right, Matt, his best friend from High School walked in through the kitchen door.

"Hey there, buddy," Matt said, looking at the comical sight. "Julie let me in and told me you were out here. Like you'd be anywhere else." He let out a mocking wolf whistle. "Whoa, nice look."

"It's what all floaters wear these days," Andrew said. "You should try it sometime. Pretty soon, everyone will be wearing this. You don't want to be the last one on your block to be sporting one!"

"Floaters?" Matt asked. "Sounds like a dead person in a river. No thanks. I'll just watch you and have my finger on the emergency button on my phone. The paramedics have your house number memorized, right?"

"Ha ha," Andrew replied. "Very funny. I'm talking about people who float in the air, and no, they don't have it memorized!"

"Like lying on your back in the pool?"

"What?"

"Sorry. I'm back on the whole floater thing. You're going to lay down and float in the air?"

"Not really," Andrew said, "more like using magnetic lines of force to float on air while standing up."

Matt had known Andrew for a long time. He knew that his sense of humor was lost on this serious scientist. "Uh-huh. You've been playing with that two hundred-thousand-volt wand, right?"

"No, I'm serious," Andrew replied. "I've been working on levitating small objects. Now, I'm ready to try something a little bigger. Are you ready?"

"Me?" Matt replied. "No, no. Not me. If you're going to levitate anything, it will be you. Like I said. 9-1-1 is just a button away. I'm here for you, bud, but not here for you to strap into a strange-looking outfit and try to float me in the air."

Just then, Julie walked out into the garage with the video camera.

"Okay, Andrew," she said, smiling. "I'm ready. Going to float for me?"

"Oh, that really doesn't sound right," Matt said. "Should I leave? What kind of video are you making, buddy?"

"Ha, ha," Andrew said. "Very funny. Stay!" He turned to Julie and said, "Yeah, if you're ready."

"At the risk of sounding dense, ready for what?"

Andrew smiled at Matt and said, "Ready for this…"

Julie started to videotape as Andrew pushed the button on the black box. A glow began to surround Andrew, initially intensifying but then dimmed some. Andrew started to rise off the ground and float in the air. In a dramatic flair, Andrew tried to spread his arms but lost his balance. He dropped the black box and returned rudely to the ground with a thud. "Ow!" he roared. "I think I cracked my tailbone! At the very least, I won't be sitting much for the next few days."

CHAPTER 7

Illusions

Matt looked at Andrew. As was a recent and frequent occurrence, he couldn't close his mouth, and nothing came out. He started to clap slowly, obviously not as impressed as Andrew would have hoped for. "That was pretty cool. So you're learning to be a magician, huh? You gonna be the next Criss Angel?"

Andrew stared at Matt in disbelief. "Magician? No! It has nothing to do with magic and everything to do with science and hard work!"

"Oh. Okay. Sorry," Matt put his index finger up to his mouth and looked around. "I know how you magician types are. You prefer to call them illusions."

Andrew ran his fingers through his hair. "It has nothing to do with magic and is not an illusion."

Matt shrugged. "Okay, buddy. Whatever you say. I've just seen things like this on TV a million times. Where are the wires?"

"No! Not whatever I say. There are no wires! It's real. I floated in the air utilizing the earth's magnetic field." Andrew's voice was rising, and so was his blood pressure.

Matt again placed a finger to his lips. "Shhhhhhhh. Remember, a good magician never gives away his secrets."

Andrew put his hand on his forehead and rubbed as if fighting off a headache. "You're driving me crazy with this talk about magic secrets."

"And speaking of secrets, what's with the stake out?" Matt looked from Andrew to Julie and back again. Both were very quiet and looked as if all knowledge had been drained from their heads.

"Stakeout?" Andrew asked.

"Yeah," Matt said. "The conspicuous green van sitting across the street. It's been there most of the morning. Didn't you see it when you got home this morning? Boy, I'll tell you what, that driver couldn't take his eyes off the house."

Andrew stared in disbelief at his friend. "What are you talking about? I didn't see any van sitting in the street this morning. Oh, wait, I remember a dark green van just up the road. But the windows were tinted. How could you see that anyone was inside?"

Matt pulled out a pair of sunglasses from his shirt pocket

and smiled. "The latest in cool shades, my friend. Let's you video, access the Internet, and see clearly through tinted glass."

Andrew realized that he was staring at Matt again. He seemed to stare at Matt in disbelief more often than he should. "I'm sure that van must be gone by now."

"Nope," Matt said, putting the sunglasses away.

"Why would anyone want to watch me?"

Matt smiled at Andrew. "Open the garage."

Andrew looked at Matt again like he was crazy. "I'm not going to open the garage. Do you see what I'm wearing? Do you see all of this equipment? If someone is watching me, and I'm not saying there is, then I don't want them seeing everything in here."

"Then you believe me about the stakeout?" Matt asked.

"Not in the least."

"Then humor me and open the door. If there's no one there, no harm done. If someone is there, we may need to start planning what to do." Matt loved chess and was pretty good at it. He knew that Andrew was smart but was a horrible chess player. It was one of the only things that Matt could beat his friend at. So when he saw the opportunity, he jumped at it. He sensed a checkmate coming on.

"Fine," Andrew reluctantly agreed and opened the garage door.

He stared out of the garage and across the street where a dark green van sat with dark-tinted windows. It was hard to tell if anyone was inside, but Andrew didn't feel right about it. As he stared and thought, Kota, their 18-year-old neighbor and babysitter, walked up the sidewalk and to the garage.

"Hey, Mr. B," Kota said, bouncing up the driveway. "What are you guys doing?"

Andrew continued to stare at the van, unsure of what to do or think. "Uh, hey, Kota."

"How come the cops are watching your house?" Kota asked. "Are you doing something illegal again? I hope not, because if you are, my family will get pretty upset about me coming over, hanging around here, and watching Stephanie."

"What? You noticed them, too? Illegal? I'm not doing anything illegal!"

"Floating's illegal?" Matt couldn't resist.

"No!" Andrew was trying to figure things out, but Matt wasn't helping.

"I didn't really notice them, Mr. B," Kota said casually.

"Thank goodness," Andrew sighed.

"Yeah, my mom told me about the stake out and sent me down to see what was up."

Matt muffled a laugh.

Julie shook her head.

"Your mom?" Andrew said. "Your mother knows about this?"

"Yeah. Mom went out to get the paper this morning and asked me about what you do here. I told her you tinkered with stuff and invented things. She said I should stop by and see what you've invented that had the authorities up in arms."

"She saw them here this morning? How is it that everyone knows about them but me?" Andrew was feeling lost.

"Yeah, at first she didn't want me to come over, but I told her that the cops were just being nosey, and that I should come see what the deal is. So, she agreed and told me to come over as long as I promised to stay out of trouble and give her a full report when I return."

"Well, come into the garage, and we'll all talk about this," Andrew said nervously.

As the garage door closed, the agent in the van's driver's seat lowered his binoculars. "Damn it," he said. "I couldn't get a good look at what was inside. I think we need to break in tonight and look around."

"Don't we need a warrant?" his partner questioned.

"Do these low-life scum need a warrant to commit crimes against these great United States? I don't think so. So why do we need permission to find out what's going on? For all you know, he and his little gang could create a new weapon. Oh no. We're going in tonight, and we're going to prove that this guy needs to be locked up and have the key melted down into a small nugget to be worn around some poor child's neck as a reminder that we saved them from unspeakable horrors."

His partner stared and waited until the driver's breathing returned to normal. "You really scare me sometimes." Then he put his air buds back in his ears and turned the music up.

Andrew started pacing. Matt thought how odd he looked wearing a jumpsuit and harness with receiver antenna wires dragging behind him while he paced. Andrew spoke as he walked, "That's weird. Why would they be watching me?"

"Duh, you big duh head. You just floated in the air. You've been floating things around your fricking house. You bring home stuff from universities that they don't use anymore, and no one in their right mind would need it at home, and you ask that question? Well, here's an answer for you." Matt lowered his voice and tried to emulate Count Dracula, "The government is everywhere, and they see everything. Today, they want to see you!"

Susie Montgomery, another of Andrew and Julie's friends from high school, walked into the garage from the house. She gave Julie a hug and looked at the gathering. "Hey, what's going on, guys?"

"Hey, Susie," Matt said, straightening his short frame. "You're looking particularly hot today."

"Save it, pancake," Susie said. "Didn't work yesterday and won't work today."

"Tomorrow?" Matt said hopefully.

"Doubtful," Susie said, patting him lightly on the cheek.

"So what's up, Andrew?" Susie asked.

"Hey, Susie," Andrew replied. "Just trying to figure something out."

"We were just discussing the stake out across the street," Matt said.

"You mean the green van with the two obvious people inside?" Susie asked nonchalantly.

"Yeah," Matt replied. "Got any ideas of what we should do?"

Andrew threw his hands in the air. "Am I the only one who hasn't noticed them?"

"Looks like it, sweetheart," Julie said. "But then you never leave the garage, so how would you know? Oh wait, you actually went out this morning. However, you have a one-track mind and tunnel vision when you go out. Don't worry about it, sweetheart. The good news is that you know now, and we can figure out what to do."

"She's got a point, buddy," Matt said.

Susie added, "It's tough to see what's going on in the outside world if you're not a part of it."

"Yeah. I thought seeing you standing outside the garage in the daylight was kinda weird," Kota added. "That never happens. I've always thought you need to get out in the sun more. You're like totally way too white. People need to squint to stand next to you and talk to you."

"Okay, I get it. I'll get out more, but for now, let me think for a minute," Andrew said. "This really creeps me out."

Matt, slowly moving closer to Susie with each sentence, looked at her and announced, "Andrew can float."

"What?" Susie's eyes opened wide.

"Cool!" Kota said.

"Yeah, it is pretty cool," Matt said. "Show them."

Andrew, increasingly distracted by his dilemma, suddenly looked up at what Matt had said. "What?"

"Show them how you can float," Matt insisted.

"Not now," Andrew replied.

"Aw, c'mon. It'll take your mind off things," Matt begged. "Eventually, you'll have to show the whole world."

"But, I need to figure…"

"C'mon Andrew. Show them how you can float." Julie said. Then she turned to Susie. "It is pretty awesome. He's been floating things around the house, in the air, for a few days."

Susie looked at Julie. "Wait. You've seen him floating things?"

"Yeah," Julie said, looking proudly at Andrew. "It's fun to watch when it's not sneaking up on you."

"I want to float something," Kota said. "I want to float in the air. I want to fly!'

"Like anti-gravity?" Susie asked Andrew.

"No, it's just like magnets attracting and repelling each other, only using the natural magnetic forces that we all have and aligning them with the earth's magnetic field," Andrew said.

"Show me," Susie said. "I'm having trouble understanding how our weak magnetic fields can in any way interact with the earth's magnetic field."

"Yeah. I wanna see it too!" Kota said.

Andrew sighed and picked up the black box. He looked from person to person with uncertainty. Then, he moved to where he was before and flipped the switch. Just as before, the glow surrounded him, then grew dimmer. He once again began to lift off the ground. Susie and Kota looked amazed at the feat, mouths open and speechless. They walked over and looked around Andrew as if looking for wires or something holding him up. As they stepped back, Andrew lowered himself to the ground.

Susie jumped up and down like a little kid. "That's pretty cool. Can I try it?"

Kota ran up next to Susie. "Oh! I'm next! I want to fly!"

"Uh, I don't know if you'd be ready for something like this," Andrew said to Susie. Then to Kota, "You definitely can't do this right now. If your mother found out that I let you do this, I would never stop hearing about it!"

Kota began to pout. "Aw. I can do it. How hard could it be?"

Andrew replied, "No. I don't want your mother getting mad at me if something happens to you."

"But I…" Kota searched for the words to convince Andrew to allow her this one small favor.

"No," Andrew insisted. "Not now. Not until I get some bugs worked out of it first. Besides, I've been practicing for several days, and I'm just learning how to control it. You might take off through the roof or something."

Susie walked over to Andrew and held out her hands. "Give me the harness. At least I want to try." When Andrew didn't move, Susie smiled slightly and said, "You afraid a woman's going to show you up?"

"No! I don't feel that way at all," he said, starting to feel undeserved pressure. "It has nothing to do with the fact that you're a woman. I wouldn't even let Matt try it if he wanted."

Matt looked slightly hurt and said, "Oh, I feel good about myself now! Thanks, buddy."

Andrew looked around at the people standing in the garage. "You guys are blowing this way out of proportion."

Julie walked over to Andrew and put her hand on his arm. "Just let her try, Andrew. What harm can it do?"

Andrew was quiet for a moment, all eyes watching him in

anticipation. He looked from person to person and then removed the harness in an apparent gesture of defeat. He stopped as everyone started to clap and cheer. "Oh, stop it! I'll let you do this, but don't get all mad at me if you get hurt."

Susie looked at Andrew with a sad, doe-eyed look. "Oh, Andrew. Don't be so paranoid. I'm your friend, and I'm asking you to let me do this. Besides, I couldn't do anything to you if I got hurt."

"What do you mean you couldn't do anything to me? Our friendship means more to you than a few dollars, right?"

Susie smirked as she spoke her reply. "I couldn't squeeze any money out of you. I know you don't have any."

Andrew stopped removing the harness and replied, "Hey, I've got money." Then he hesitated briefly as he glanced at Julie. "Well, Julie handles the money, but you're right. I'd only give you money at the end of the night and the sports bar when it's time to pay the bill. You'd have to fight Julie for something like this."

Susie smiled and poked Andrew's nose. "Yeah, and I would never take money from her." Susie took the harness from Andrew and started to put it on while Andrew stood speechless.

"You women all stick together, don't you?" Andrew looked on, expecting an answer.

"You know it, my friend," Matt teased. "We can't even touch the brotherhood of women."

"Don't you mean the sisterhood of women?" Andrew replied.

"Oh, come on, Andrew. Wake up and realize that women run everything. Except for the POD you haven't built yet." Matt laughed.

Julie put her arm around Susie's shoulder as they stood side by side. "If we don't come to each other's aid, who will be there for us? The big strong men?"

Andrew knew she was teasing him, but he still felt uncomfortable with the comment. "Now I feel so good about myself."

Julie approached Andrew and said, "Oh, I would never exclude you, and I'm always there for you. But you know it won't hurt to let Susie try your harness."

"I know," Andrew pouted, "and you're right."

The two looked lovingly at each other momentarily until Susie spoke up. "Alright, you two. Save it for later and tell me how to make it work."

Andrew blushed, knowing that everyone was staring. "Well, all you have to do is just stand there. When I flip this switch, you'll feel a little lightheaded. Put your chin up a little to shift your balance and you'll begin to float."

"Okay," Susie said. She stood nervously and tipped her head back slightly, waiting for something. She wasn't sure what.

"Be careful, though," Andrew cautioned. "Your balance is going to feel way off."

"Uh-huh." Susie was focused more on feeling something than listening to Andrew.

Andrew continued, "You might feel like falling, but don't bring your head forward too fast, or you will fall flat on your face."

Susie interrupted him impatiently, "This, from experience?"

"Yeah," he said distractedly. "Now, when you're about a foot off the ground…"

Susie interrupted him again but, this time, sounded irritated at his delay. "Will you just throw the switch already? Mon Dieu mon ami.   Poussez le bouton!"

"What?" Andrew didn't know French, and he knew that Susie only used it when she was getting upset.

"Just push the damn button already!"

CHAPTER 8

Lift Me Up

"Oh. Okay. Hold on." Andrew said, somewhat flustered. He quickly looked over her attachment of the harness and then flipped the switch. As before, with Andrew, a glow generated around Susie and then faded. As Susie began to lift off the ground, she had the sensation that the ground was moving away from her. At first, it was a little disconcerting, like someone had slowly opened a trap door under her, or she was on an elevator suspended in space as it rapidly descended. Once she realized it was actually her moving up, she smiled and turned her head slightly to the right. Her body moved to the right. She turned her head slightly to the left, and her body followed. She moved her feet in a walking motion, and her body moved forward a bit. She made a swimming motion in the air to help propel her forward and aid her stability. Andrew stared in amazement.

"This is pretty simple," Susie said, "and a lot of fun! Who needs diets when you can feel this light?"

Andrew was still confused and asked, "How are you doing that?"

Susie smiled to herself, then outwardly. "I can't tell you all of my secrets."

"You've never told me any of your secrets," Andrew said, still fixed on her every move.

"Bingo!" Susie said as she tilted her head far back and was suddenly upside down, nose to nose with Andrew. She winked at him and then brought her body, in a controlled motion, back to her original standing position. Once she was upright again and a mere few inches from the ground, Andrew turned off the switch, and Susie slowly floated back down. Susie took a theatrical bow as the others in the garage began to clap. "Thank you! Thank you, my adoring fans. The next show is at two o'clock. Bring roses and your friends!"

"And how did you do that!?" Andrew asked, being further astonished.

"What? The bow? It's easy. You extend your arms outward flowingly and bend at the waist."

"Not the bow," Andrew said, "When I shut it off, I fell to the ground. You floated! How did you float to the ground?"

"Did you want me to fall?" Susie asked indignantly.

"No," Andrew replied, "that's why I waited until you were right side up again."

"I really didn't do anything. I didn't even know you had turned it off until my feet touched the ground," Susie said. "I guess maybe I'm just more graceful than you are."

Matt rolled his eyes. "Show off," he said, smiling at Susie.

Susie looked coyly at Matt and said, "Thank you very much. I show off as much as I'm allowed to get away with."

Julie comforted Andrew, who was still confused, with a hug. "Maybe women just have a better sense of what to do when their balance is off. We can go through a rapid belly change, which throws off our center of gravity when we're pregnant, and you don't see many women falling down."

"Maybe I'm just a little better at handling this whole thing," Susie said as she started taking off her harness.

"What does that mean?" Andrew said, taking the comment personally.

"Oh, Andrew," Susie said, "don't be all put out. I just mean that you are so involved with everything you're doing here that you frequently look at it mechanically. On the other hand, I look at it with new eyes and don't expect anything except the experience."

"The experience?" Andrew asked. "What do you mean?"

"I look at it like, if I float, I float. You look at it in desperation. 'If I can't get this thing to work, I will be ticked off.' Do you see what I'm saying?"

Andrew did see, and it suddenly made perfect sense. It had never occurred to him, but she was right. "I never thought about it that way, but I guess I see what you're saying. And yes, a new perspective can make a world of difference. Thank you for sharing that with me. The next time I try this, I'll try it without expectation. It should be easier to do since I know that it already works. Maybe trying it while more relaxed will yield better results."

"If you mean it will be easier, I agree," Susie said, handing the harness back to Andrew. "I'm glad to see that you realize that, Andrew. The next time someone wants to help you with your experiments, like me, don't be hurt just because I could do something the first time that you couldn't. We all have different abilities and see things in different ways."

Having been silent for too long, Matt chimed in, "And speaking of seeing things in different ways, what do you want to do about the van across the street?"

Everyone turned and looked at Matt, just a little confused. Matt was accustomed to seeing that type of look from his friends, which didn't surprise him. He just continued to look from person to person, waiting for an answer. "Well?" he said.

Susie broke the silence, "What does that have to do with anything we were talking about?"

"I dunno," Matt shrugged. "It made sense in my mind."

Andrew said, "Strange as it sounds, he's right. We can't all stay in here for the next week. Let me think." Andrew started pacing again. "Do you really think they're watching me?"

"Again, as before, buddy, Duh!" Matt said.

"Do you think they're spying on me to see what I'm doing in here?" Andrew stated to no one in particular.

Matt started to answer, "Once again, buddy…"

"Shut up, Matt!" He stopped talking, intimidated by everyone speaking the exact words in unison.

Julie spoke up, "Maybe. You are coming up with some pretty interesting things that, I'm sure, the government would want to know about, or maybe even some other government. I haven't thought about that until now, but what if those guys across the street aren't even from our government? What if they're foreign spies?"

Kota said timidly, "Well then, maybe you should just show them."

Everyone turned to Kota and stared. She took a small step back, suddenly becoming the center of attention.

Matt thought he knew where this was going, but for the benefit of everyone else there, he asked, "What are you talking about? What's your thinking on this?"

"Well, if they want to see what you're doing, they'll probably figure out how to do it on their own terms, right? But if you just showed them before they're ready, it might take them by surprise."

"You know," Andrew started, "I think Kota's on to something. Maybe we should just let them know what we're doing. Give them a show."

Matt held up his hands and took a step back. "What do you mean 'we' kimosabe? If the government is going to get involved, I don't want to be implicated. Remember Nixon? Even he couldn't fight the government and was a big part of it."

"Don't worry, Matt," Andrew said, walking over and touching Matt's shoulder. "It'll be good. Here's my plan."

Andrew gathered everyone in a huddle and explained what he wanted to do. Everyone laughed and nodded.

"Let's do this!" Andrew said.

The driver of the van was trying his hardest not to nod off.

"There hasn't been any activity in hours other than a few friends coming by and disappearing into the house," he grumbled to his partner. "I don't think of them as friends of the family. They're probably co-conspirators. Whatever reason these people have to visit can't be good or friendly. It had to be with the intent of overthrowing the government somehow. The government that we have sworn to be faithful to with oaths to uphold no matter what the cost."

"Did you say something?" His partner asked, pulling the air pods out of his ears.

"Help me stay awake!" He mentally slapped himself in the face and woke up to the realization that the garage door was, once again, opening.

At first, he sat up, and then he scrunched down so as not to be seen. He knew that the tinted windows were dark enough, but human reaction sometimes took over, even though he didn't want to admit it. "Get down!" he told his partner.

"What?"

The driver pointed. "Don't let them see you."

The other agent shook his head and watched.

Julie ducked underneath the still-opening door, holding a video camera. She ran to the end of the driveway, picked up the camera, and pointed it at the garage.

The two agents watched, transfixed, and wondered what would happen.

The first agent, trying to still look inconspicuous, nudged his partner. "Looks like we have some activity."

"Do you think we should call it in?" he replied.

"No, I do not. Not now. Let's see what happens. It may be a trick. Look at the woman with the camera. The wife. She seems a little too enthused about this." As the two agents looked on, the driver's eyes grew wider than they should have. "What the hell…? What is that? Do you see that?"

The agent in the passenger seat craned to see what was

going on, but a tree branch was in the way. "What? What are you seeing?"

The driver pointed, looking like he had seen a ghost. "That!" The passenger looked under the branch. He saw Andrew walking out of the garage. He was wearing the harness, holding the black box, and walking about a foot off the ground. The agents sat in the van, mouths agape, not wanting to take their eyes off Andrew. Not able to do so! Andrew turned and started walking down the street toward the van. The agents, transfixed by the site, sat motionless as Andrew approached the van.

When he reached the van, he turned off the black box and floated gently to the ground, thanks to Susie's advice. He smiled broadly and tapped on the window.

The two agents looked at each other. The passenger shrugged and said, "You're the head agent here. You wanted to see what was going on. Maybe you should see what he wants."

"Wipe that smirk off your face. Stay calm. It might be a trap of some kind." He rolled down the window. "May I help you, sir?"

"Hey, guys. What's up, besides me?" Andrew chuckled at his own joke. "Couldn't help but notice you've been watching me all day. Is there anything I can help you with?"

The agent didn't answer at first but then shook his head and started to stammer his reply, "I don't know what you're talking about. We, uh, just stopped here for some lunch because of this, uh, tree. Yeah, it's giving us some shade. You really startled me, you know. I didn't even see you floating toward the van, I mean, walking up to the van. Yeah, I guess it looked like you were floating with the heat and everything. You know, one of those optical illusions like the water on the road that's not water. Floating. What was I thinking?" He laughed.

The agent in the passenger seat could hardly contain himself.

Andrew chuckled, "I know. You probably don't see people floating in the air every day, do you? It's fun. You should try it sometime."

The agent, once again speechless, shook his head slightly.

"Well, that's okay," Andrew continued. "I'm not quite used to it yet, either. But you know what they say, 'practice makes perfect.'"

The agent nodded in agreement.

Andrew was amused with himself. He had never done anything like this, and it felt pretty good. "Well, I came over here because you guys have been sitting here all day, and my wife is about ready to make lunch. We were wondering if you would like a sandwich or something. She makes a mean PB&J. I might even be able to find you guys a soda or something. What do you say? My treat. You said you were stopping for lunch, but I don't see any food out. With such a long lunch hour and no food, you guys must be starving."

Still dumbstruck, the agent didn't say anything for a

moment or two but shook his head, still staring in disbelief. "Uh, no thanks. We've got a lunch."

Andrew had to get one more shot in: "Are you sure? It's really no problem. We don't have much, but we're happy to share."

The driver continued to stare and said, "No, uh, thanks anyway."

"Okay. Suit yourselves." Andrew flipped the switch on his box and lifted, again, off the ground. He floated to the other side of the street as Julie continued to film. The two agents watched on in amazement. Once Andrew returned to the garage, Julie stopped recording, looked over toward the van, and blew a kiss. She smiled and hurried back to the garage. The driver continued to sit there with a look of confusion on his face. He shook his head again, rolled the window up, and turned to his partner.

"Did you get any of that on video?" he asked urgently. "Did you take any pictures?"

"Uh, no sir," he answered. "I didn't think about turning on my body cam. Besides, I could barely see with this tree limb in the way. Did you? Take any pictures, I mean."

"You didn't think about it?" the driver asked angrily.

"No," he repeated. "And again, did you?"

The driver looked back out the window and then back at the passenger. He looked down, embarrassed. "No."

"What are we going to tell headquarters?" the passenger asked.

"I don't know," he said. "I just don't know. They'll never believe this. Maybe we should report nothing to see and go home."

"Yeah," the passenger responded. "I think you're right. Let's just go home. I haven't seen my wife in a few days and want a shower."

The driver shot the passenger a dirty look, started the van, and they drove off.

Back in the garage, a celebration of relief was underway. Everyone smiled, laughed, congratulated each other, and talked about things from their point of view.

"Did you see the look on his face?" Matt laughed.

"I thought he was going to throw up," Susie said. "The only way it could have been better is if I were standing at the window with you, but you did a great job, Andrew. You were the right one to go."

"Thanks, Susie," Andrew said as he removed the harness.

Julie laughed, "I'm glad I got that on tape. It was the funniest thing I've ever seen."

"That was way cool, Mr. B.," Kota said. "Even if I didn't get to try it. I get to try it now, though, right? I mean, you've tried it out, and you know it works, and Susie got to try it out, and she was really good with it, and I really want to try it out, please, please, please, Mr. B."

"We'll have to remedy that, Kota. Maybe not today, but soon. Like tomorrow, how about that?" Andrew said.

Kota squealed in delight. "I can't wait to tell my friends!"

"Hold on there," Andrew said, raising his hands. "Let's not get carried away with telling the world yet. I want to finish a few other things before the world finds out what I've been doing."

"But," Kota pouted, "it was so cool, and the whole thing today was pretty funny."

"Yes, it was cool and pretty funny. And what a rush! I can't believe I did that. I'm still shaking a little."

Julie approached Andrew and said, "I can believe you did it. You can do anything!" She turned him toward her and gave him a big kiss. Everyone made the sounds indicating that they should knock it off and save it for later.

The five continued to laugh at the adventure as Andrew finished taking off the harness.

Suddenly, there was an awkward silence.

"So, what now?" Susie asked, breaking the silence.

CHAPTER 9

Decisions

"What do you mean?" Andrew asked.

"What do you do with this?" she continued. "Do we all now learn to fly like superheroes? Does this replace planes and cars?"

"Whoa, whoa, whoa!" Andrew said, holding up his hands. "I'm unsure if the world is ready to take off into the wild blue yonder yet and compete with our feathered friends. No, not yet. First, I want to amplify and use it in my POD."

"Your what?" Susie asked. "POD? What is a POD?"

"A little behind the times, aren't you?" Matt said, walking over to Susie. "Maybe we could go out for coffee or a quick bite, and I could fill you in?"

"Okay. Sure," Susie purred.

"Really?" Matt said excitedly.

"No," Susie replied, tagging his nose with her index finger.

"Ah. Rejected again," Matt said. "But at least you touched me. We're making progress!"

Susie sighed.

"You two crack me up!" Andrew said. "But about the POD. It's a device that I'm building that we can travel in."

"Travel where?" Matt asked.

"Anywhere you want," Andrew replied.

"Like, to the Bahamas?" Matt asked.

"If you want," Andrew said.

"To France?" Susie enquired.

"Definitely!"

Kota asked, "To a concert in Japan?"

"Why not?" said Andrew.

"To the moon?" Julie asked.

At this, everyone fell silent and turned to look at Andrew, who also was far too quiet. He dropped his head, thinking about what Julie had just said, and then he looked up. "You know," he said, still thinking about it, "we probably could."

Everyone, somewhat silent because of the question,

became deathly silent because of the answer. Matt was the first to speak up.

"So, what do you mean by that, buddy?" Matt wasn't sure he wanted to hear the answer, although the thought of space travel had always intrigued him.

"Well," Andrew started, still deep in thought and more thinking out loud, "we couldn't when the moon was on the sun side of the earth, but when it's on the dark side, the solar winds drive the magnetosphere out and around the moon, bathing it in the magnetic lines from the earth. We could, theoretically, follow those lines all the way to the moon."

"What about beyond the moon?" Julie asked quietly.

Andrew again thought about the question. Everyone was again silent, waiting for an answer. "You know what's funny?" he said, "I've looked into the magnetic lines of force throughout the solar system, and there is an interplanetary network that almost connects the planets."

"So, what are you saying?" Matt asked. "We could go out beyond the moon?

"I'm not really sure at this point," Andrew said. "I'm pretty certain we could, but first, I'll have to conduct some research. Besides, my POD isn't really designed for space travel. I was only thinking about time travel when I put it together."

"Time travel?" Susie asked, her eyes getting wide. "So we could travel back and see the birth of the universe? But would it be possible? Isn't it only theory and a rather sketchy one at that?”

Kota said, “It would be nice if I could go back and see firsthand the history assignments I get in school!”

“Whoa, whoa, slow down,” Andrew said, “I don’t even know if it will work on this type of scale.”

“But, theoretically, it’s possible, right Andrew?” Julie asked.

“Maybe,” Andrew said, “and maybe not. Let’s take it one step at a time.”

“Well, hurry up and find out,” Susie said impatiently. “There are so many things I would love to do if I went back in time.”

“That’s another thing we must think about, though,” Andrew cautioned. “If we change one thing in time, how would it affect other things?”

“You mean like the ripple effect?” Susie said. “I’ve read things about that.”

“Oh, now, where have you read things about time travel?” Matt asked.

“I read a number of different things about several different topics, Matt, and if you weren’t so wrapped up in yourself or in pursuing me, then maybe you would know that.”

Andrew’s first reaction was to point at Matt and yell, “Burn!” but he was more involved in the conversation. He’d save it for another day. "Yeah, Susie. I am talking about the ripple effect. So many theories piled on top of each other."

"So what exactly is the ripple effect, Andrew?" Julie asked.

Andrew said, "It's a theory that says if you change one thing in time, no matter how small, it ripples out like a pebble thrown into a pond."

"Now you just sound like Confucius." Matt huffed.

"No, really, it's a real theory," Andrew said. "It just means that if we travel through time, we must be careful about what we do."

"Actually, buddy, any theory can be a real one. Based on speculation, educated guessing, and research of what is real. I could make up some theories, but I'd rather have fun. So let's just say that, hopefully, we won't mess things up too much." Matt grinned.

Kota was excited now. "You mean we're going through time?"

"We?" Andrew knew that this was getting a little out of hand. "I don't know about all of us. I guess I could build a bigger POD."

"We could all help!" Susie said excitedly.

Kota looked down, "I don't know anything about building a POD."

"But I'm sure we could all find something to do to help,"

Susie said, smiling at Kota. I've never built a POD either, and you know what? I don't think Andrew has either." She looked at Andrew and realized that everyone was looking at him.

Andrew looked from person to person and said, "I think, if you're all willing, we could work together to make it happen."

They all gathered and spoke excitedly with each other, agreeing to meet the next day back in the garage and begin planning and working on the POD.

Just after the last person entered the house, a faint voice could be heard in the quiet of the empty garage. The first voice was harsh and evil sounding.

"Do you remember the time tremor we felt last week?"

The second voice sounded fearful and trembled slightly.

"Yes?"

The first voice continued, "I believe I've pinpointed it."

"Where did it come from?"

The first voice was now sounding not only evil but also impatient. "Dimension 419B."

"I'll begin focusing my search there, find out why it happened, and let you know."

"Don't let me down," the first voice threatened. "I must have the secret."

CHAPTER 10

Upside Down

We grow up with specific rules instilled in us. We learn what is right and wrong according to these rules. When we do what is considered wrong, we are, at first, disciplined by others and then, as we get older, by our own conscience. What if we entered a world where right and wrong differed from what we've learned? How would we react to such a world? How would we be received in such a world? In our world, a visitor who does not honor our beliefs might be scorned or jailed. How would we fare in a world where all values seem to have gone askew? ~ Andrew Barton

"Every week seems to drag by more slowly than the one before," Andrew said, plopping into a chair. "I wish we could start making money from my discoveries so I could quit working for the warehouse, but I would have no idea who would be safe to tell or share with."

"It will all come together, Andrew," Julie said, putting dinner on the table.

"I don't even know what good any of this would do," he said.

Julie stood behind him and rubbed his shoulders. "Andrew, I know you're frustrated and tired from working. Your ten-hour shifts are tough and tiring. You only have to believe in yourself the way I do. It will come, and when that time arrives, we'll know. Just keep doing what you do; it will make us and the world richer."

Andrew reached back and squeezed Julie's hand. "I love you," he said.

"Let's eat dinner and get to bed. You have an early Friday and, hopefully, an energetic Friday evening. I can't wait to see what you do this weekend!"

Andrew was eager to see what the weekend would hold as well!

Andrew was up with the sun. Julie wasn't as eager to get up but always found Andrew's excitement infectious. After a quick breakfast, Andrew hurried toward the garage.

"What are you working on today?" Julie asked.

"Wait until you see it. It's almost finished," Andrew said excitedly.

"The POD?" Julie asked.

"Exactly!" Andrew said. "Come out in a little while and

take a look at it. I have to review a few circuits inside, and then we can see what it does!"

Andrew kissed Julie and bounded out the door into the garage.

The curious contraption was built with Andrew's own two hands and the generous help of his wife and friends. The outside was not pretty but was a composite of wood and metal with a small door just large enough for one person to squeeze through.

Andrew was inside, working on various lights, wires, circuits, and, of course, magnets. He knelt in the cramped space and then tried to sit. Then Andrew squashed down as far as he could to reach under the panel. He felt gingerly around the wires and wriggled various plugs. *Ah ha*, Andrew thought to himself, finding the loose connection. He carefully felt around with the one hand that could reach and worked it back up. He sat up and pushed a button. The panel lit up, and gauges began to flicker. "She's not a beauty, but she'll fly me to the nearest port in the storm," he said to no one there. No one he could see, anyway.

"You're not talking about me, are you?" Julie had appeared in the doorway of the POD.

"Never!" he said in his best pirate voice. "Argh, you're the finest wench I've found, and I'd be taking you with me over the seven seas and beyond."

"Yeah, yeah," she said, laughing, "whatever you say, Black Beard. So what are you doing out here?"

"Just finishing up a few things before I take her for a test drive," Andrew said.

"Can I drive it?" Kota stuck her head in the doorway.

"Not until I make sure it's safe," Andrew said sternly.

"Aw," Kota pouted.

"It's not you," Andrew said. "I'm not even letting Julie drive it."

Julie folded her arms and squinted her eyes.

"Yet," Andrew continued. "Look, I'm not even sure what it's going to do or what it's capable of doing. Right now, I just want to see if I can get it to float."

"Yeah, and that reminds me," Kota said, "I never got my turn to float."

"Oh yeah," Andrew said. "I'm sorry. I'll get the harness out for you as soon as I'm done testing this."

Kota smiled broadly and clapped her hands. "Yay!"

"So, what are your plans with this today, Andrew?" Julie asked.

"I just want to see if I can get it to float about a foot off the ground," he said, "with me inside."

"Isn't that a lot of weight?" Julie asked, continuing with her questioning. "Between you and the amount of wood and metal we've used, we can hardly move it in the garage. You should put some wheels on the bottom later if we have to move it somewhere."

"When you're dealing with the lines of force interacting with each other, the weight of an object really doesn't matter. What matters is how strong the lines of force are in any given object and how those lines interact with the lines of objects around it."

"Uh huh," Julie said. She looked at Kota, who just offered a weak smile.

"Can I see inside?" Kota asked.

"I don't see why not," Andrew said. "You can both come in, and I'll show you around.

The two women stepped into the small enclosure and looked around. They were more impressed by the blinking lights and wires than by the creature comforts.

"Once you get this thing working," Julie said, "we'll have to work on making it a little more comfortable. Doesn't look like it would be very appealing on long trips."

"That's the beauty of it," Andrew said. "It won't take that long, or it shouldn't take that long, to get anywhere we want to go."

"What do you mean?" Kota asked. "Isn't distance, well, distance?"

"It is," Andrew replied. "But look at it this way. Walking from point A to point B, I get there in a certain amount of time. If I run the same distance, I get there faster. But, if I go that same distance following the magnetic lines of force, I can get there instantaneously."

"Huh? I'm confused. How can you get anywhere instantaneously?"

"Look at where you are now," Andrew continued, "you're just standing here, but you're traveling simultaneously. You're traveling through time. Each second that goes by takes you from point A to point B in time. But because you're not moving, you're reaching that destination instantaneously. Now, if you could suspend time around you and move, say, from the POD to the kitchen, then start time again, to you, it would have taken a minute or two, but to those around you, it would be immediate. And because you've suspended time, you wouldn't have aged."

"So you're manipulating time while you're moving?" Julie asked.

"I hope so. I hope the little accident a few weeks ago can be controlled. We'll find out. But first, I need to see if I can get this thing to float. It will help me to see if my theory on weight works. So out with you. I'll need you to record what happens from the outside." Andrew gave Julie and Kota a mock push toward the door. As he did, Kota lost her balance and accidentally grabbed a panel while trying to catch herself. All the lights dimmed momentarily, flickered, and then came back on.

As Kota looked around at everything happening, her face twisted in horror. "I'm so sorry, Mr. B. I broke it!"

"Oh, Kota," Andrew said, trying to console her, "you didn't break anything. I've been dealing with loose connections all day. Don't worry," Andrew said, "it will be fine."

"No. I know I did something wrong." Kota was almost in tears.

"I'm sure you didn't do anything, Kota," Julie said, putting her arm around Kota's shoulders. "If Andrew says it's fine, then it is. Let's leave the POD and let Andrew do his test."

Kota and Julie stepped out of the POD and turned to look at Andrew. "Are you coming out, or will you try now?"

"No time like the present!" Andrew said, smiling. "I'll shut the door and give it a try. Could you video what happens on the outside so I can see it afterward?"

"Okay," said Julie. "When do you want me to turn on the camera?"

"Give me about two minutes after I close the door, then start recording. I shouldn't be in there more than five minutes," Andrew said.

"Five of your minutes, or five of my minutes?" Julie asked jokingly.

Andrew didn't get the joke.

"I'll see you in a few," Julie said. Andrew closed the door, and Julie heard it latch.

"Come back to me," she whispered, turning to get the camera.

"I have a peculiar feeling," Kota said.

"Me too," Julie said.

Inside the POD, Andrew began reviewing his checklist. He quickly increased the power once he was satisfied that everything was ready.

When I improve this thing, he thought, *I really need to put in some windows. The view is nothing to brag about!*

The magnetic generator worked well, generating as much voltage and magnetic flux as he had hoped. He watched the plasma container as it started to glow. Andrew felt the lightheaded feeling he always had when floating with the harness. Then came the 'thump'. He wasn't sure what it was, and it only concerned him a bit, at first, anyway. The more he thought about it, the more he needed to know what had happened. Did someone hit the outside of the POD? Did the magnetism attract something, causing damage to the POD? The errant thoughts flooded his mind, so he shut everything down and opened the door to the POD.

Andrew was a little more than surprised when very bright light flooded into the interior of the POD. Once his eyes adjusted, he saw Julie standing outside the POD, her arms folded. Andrew realized the POD was in the driveway and no longer in the garage. It was a confusing situation, and Andrew needed answers. He stepped out and walked over to Julie. "How did the POD get out here?"

"Andy," she said, "can we please be done with this stupid POD crap. It did nothing. It sat there. It's like a little sweatbox. And thank God that none of our friends were here when you went in, waving like the Queen of England to her subjects. Our friends and neighbors talk about and ridicule you every day. Do you know that? I wish you had built this in the backyard, at the very least. So embarrassing"

Andrew stared at her. "What are you talking about?"

"Oh, my God! And now you'll tell me you forgot our entire conversation a few minutes ago? Remember the one we had before you decided to sulk in your stupid little POD? It's like a kids' clubhouse. The next time you want to sulk, just come inside and sulk in the bedroom like a normal adult would. Or go to the bar. Anything but coming out to the wooden monstrosity. If we're lucky, maybe lightning will strike it, and it will burn to the ground."

Andrew stepped back. "I really don't know what you're talking about. I went into the POD a few minutes ago and was in a great mood when it was in the garage. I wasn't sulking. I was celebrating my accomplishments. You and Kota were standing outside of it, in the garage, and you were going to video what happened when I tried to levitate it."

"Kota and I?" Julie's eyes narrowed. "Do you have alcohol inside that thing? Is that how you were celebrating?" She smelled his breath.

"I have not been drinking. Why would I drink while experimenting? And why would I drink in front of Kota?"

"And that's another thing. Are you fantasizing about Kota? You know she only comes over on Thursdays for sex training. Why would she be here today? If you want to take things to the next level with her, it's fine, but this isn't how to do it, Andy. Is that what this is about? Shall we talk to her during the next sex session?"

"The next what!?" Andrew was speechless at this point. His head was spinning. Something was not right at all.

"Andy, what is wrong with you?"

Andrew looked around, waiting to wake up from a horrible dream. "Why do you keep calling me 'Andy'?"

"Um, let's see, maybe because it's your name? What is going on with you? Did you hit your head or something while you were in there? Are you sure you haven't been drinking?"

Julie reached out to feel his forehead. Her touch was soft and cool. It was Julie's touch. It was Julie's body and voice. He looked around. It was his house. He looked up and saw Susie crossing the street. Maybe she'll know what's going on.

"Hey Andy," Susie said in a low and sexy tone. She took his right hand and put his index finger in her mouth. He was shocked and immediately pulled his hand away, looking at Julie. She looked furious. Andrew decided that, perhaps, Susie didn't know what was going on. Susie pouted at first but then smiled. "Will this be a 'hard to get' night? I kind of like that thought," she purred. "We haven't tried that in a few months, and as I recall, it was one of our best nights ever." Susie reached up and gently scratched Andrews's face and smiled.

"Why did you do that?' Julie asked in a furious voice?

"Are you talking to me?" Andrew asked. "Why did I do what?" He was beginning to feel like the whole world had turned upside down.

"Why did you pull your hand away like that? Today is Saturday, or did you forget that little fact too?" Julie stared at him, waiting for a reply from Andrew, who didn't have one. Then she turned to Susie. "I am so sorry, Susie. I don't know what's gotten into Andy today." Julie gave Susie a passionate kiss. "But I still love you," Julie said to Susie. "We'll get things straightened out by tonight." Julie shot a glance at Andrew. "Won't we, Andy?"

"It's okay, Julie," Susie said. "Matthew told me that Andy had been acting strange lately, but I didn't expect him to be rude. Maybe I'll ask Matthew to come over and chat with him. Sometimes, the guys tell each other things they don't tell us."

"Better make it quick, Susie," Julie said. "I'm about ready to kill him now."

"Don't kill him," Susie purred. "He's great in bed, and better once we all get going. We'll get it all figured out." Susie blew Andrew a kiss, trotted off across the street, and entered the house immediately across from theirs."

"I can't believe you." Julie turned and stomped into the house. Andrew followed. Inside, Julie flopped down on the couch. Andrew carefully sat next to her.

"I'm sorry," he started. "I really don't know what's going on."

"You don't know what's going on?" Julie asked in an irritated tone. "It's the same thing that goes on every Saturday. You've always loved it. I've always loved it. Our partners have always loved it. And now you insult Susie?"

"Okay, now see, you've lost me again. Our partners?" Andrew's head was spinning.

"Our daily sex partners. Matthew and Susie have been our married Saturday partners for 10 years." Julie sounded nonchalant but annoyed.

Andrew sat, stunned and numb. He didn't even know what to say. Julie spoke, but Andrew, lost in thought and trying to figure out what happened this time, didn't hear her words. "Andy!" Julie snapped her fingers in front of his face. "You look like you're going to throw up. Are you sick?"

"I'm not sick," Andrew said, "but I'm not alright either. Somehow, I must have slipped into another dimension."

"Oh, here we go," Julie said, throwing her hands into the air. She was greatly relieved when Matt walked in through the front door. "Oh, Matthew," Julie said and ran over to him. They gave each other a brief kiss. "I sure as hell hope that you can straighten him out."

"I'll try," Matt said, walking over to sit beside Andrew. "Hey, buddy," Matt said, touching Andrew's shoulder. "What's going on? The girls tell me you've been acting a little loony since you entered the POD. Want to tell me what happening inside that head of yours?" Matt sniffed at Andrew and pulled back slightly. "Andy? What's different about you?"

CHAPTER 11

No Place Like Home

Andrew pulled back a little. "Why are you sniffing me?"

"Andy usually wears a different cologne than what I'm smelling. No offense, but his is better. I gave it to him."

Andrew turned to Matt. "Look, Matt…"

"Whoa now, Andy," Matt looked sternly at his friend. "If we're going to work this out, then we need to stop going there with the 'Matt' calling. It's always been Matthew, and it always will be."

"I'm sorry, Matthew. What do you know about what I've been trying to do with my POD?" Andrew started.

"Uh, nothing more than what you've told me. Inter-dimensional shifting and time displacement. Why? Thinking of something else that you need my help with?" Matthew sat quietly.

"Did you say inter-dimensional shifting?" Andrew thought that this dimension's 'Andy' did it. Andy was working with the shifting and accidentally activated his POD at the same time Andrew activated his. They must have somehow switched places.

"Yeah. Why? What's going on, Andy?" Matt sounded genuinely concerned but almost sounded like a psychiatrist.

"Matt, uh, Matthew. I want to tell you something, and I want you to listen. Something is going on that you need to know."

"Okay. I'm listening. Let's get to the bottom of this."

"Matt, uh, Matthew, about half an hour ago, I was entering my POD, but it was in my garage. Julie, my Julie, was also there getting ready to video my most recent attempt to make the POD lift off the ground. When I ramped up the power, I felt a thump. I powered down, opened the door, and was suddenly in the driveway and in this dimension. I'm guessing your Andrew here, in this world, activated his POD at the same time, and somehow, we switched places."

"So, you're telling me that you're not the Andy I have known since Sex Ed classes? Let's find out. I will ask you a few questions about 'your world' and talk to you about 'our world,' and we'll look at the differences. Is that okay?"

"Good idea. Ask away!"

"Okay. Tell me what you know about me."

"Let's see," Andrew started, "you and I have known each other all our lives. You were the state champion wrestler in high school. You hate fish and love rare steaks. You've been chasing Susie for years but can't seem to convince her that getting together is a good idea. Julie and I have been married for ten years. We have a daughter named Stephanie…"

"What do you mean we have a daughter?"

"Stephanie," Andrew said. "She's the love of our

lives."

Matt looked concerned. "Andy, I believe your story. You really struck a nerve with Julie just now, and there is no way that our Andy would say anything like that. Here, in this place, you and Julie have a child, but like all children, you were never told the sex of that child and didn't name it."

Andrew looked horrified. "What?"

"Now I'm convinced even more. Let me tell you about where you are now. In our world, when a female child is born, they receive an implant that controls the ovaries and uterus and their functions. Men receive a similar implant that makes sperm dormant. Women can only get pregnant by petitioning the government. When the government approves, her implant is switched off. Then she picks her bio partner, and his is also deactivated. Both are temporary. Most women choose not to do this, as they then have to deal with menstruation, cramps, and the whole messy, unpleasant thing. Once a woman becomes pregnant, and after the child is born, the government takes it to one of the many growth facilities, where it's named, raised, and educated. Because sex is a primal emotion, in 1922, congress passed an amendment to the Constitution saying that sex is a God-given right, and the Freedom of Sex Act was enacted. Because sex is such a common thing with only minimal boundaries, there are no more sex crimes. Our society worldwide has become more relaxed and more productive. There are still a few odd groups that hold out, claiming that monogamy is the way to go, and Utah is one of the biggest. It has several offshoots of religious factions that claim monogamy is the only way to live. They still live the way people did a hundred years ago. Poor women, going through that misery every month. Not to mention menopause." Julie made an audible and unpleasant sound. Andrew smiled to himself. "So," Matthew continued, "around age 14, boys and girls are given sex education. At 16, the government helps them find jobs and places to live until they are 18. Then, they should be on their own. Many, like Kota, find local couples to help with their partner training."

"What about jealousy?" Andrew asked.

Matthew laughed. "This has been a way of life for us for almost 100 years. Some people still do get jealous, but those people just choose to not get married or find someone who wants monogamy. Or they move to Utah," he said, smiling. "But seriously, we could sit here all day and discuss our society and your society, but I believe we need to find a way to send you back and retrieve our Andy. I can't imagine that you, with your thoughts on how things should be, would ever make it in our world. Heaven help our Andy in your world right now. If he has any intelligence, he'll stay in the POD until we can get this figured out." Once Matthew realized what he had said, he looked at Julie. "Oh god, Julie," Matthew said. "What has he done? We have got to get him back here as soon as possible!"

"Yes. Please!" Julie insisted.

The three wandered outside and over to the POD. Andrew and Matt opened the door and looked inside. Andrew spoke up as Matthew started to write down numbers from the panel readings. "Since I made the trip here, perhaps I should be the one to take the readings and set the destination for going back."

Matthew turned and looked at him in disbelief. "Look, Andy. You have been messing around with this against my warnings and better judgment for months. You've really screwed things up. I told you to quit messin' with things you don't understand, but as usual, you wouldn't listen to me. After you got zapped by that stupid two hundred-thousand volt wand of yours, I thought you'd listen to me, but noooooo."

Andrew was a little taken aback by this statement and somewhat offended. "I got zapped? As I recall, I had to tell you to stop playing with it before you got zapped."

Matthew put down the notepad and turned threateningly toward Andrew. He glared and said, "In your world?"

Andrew calmed down a bit at this statement and remembered where he was. "Yeah. In my world. In my world, Matt is a great guy and a good friend, but he tends to be a little off the wall sometimes. I'm sorry, I forgot where I was."

Matthew softened and replied, "Yeah, well, you're in my world now. And in my world, Andy is the one who's a little 'off the wall.'"

Andrew chuckled, "It's amazing how the timelines differ. You see, I think what happened is that..."

"Save it for your Matthew," Matthew interrupted. "I could probably tell you more about time travel and inter-dimensional theory than you've ever known existed. Your dimension is just a different timeline than ours. A different sequence of events that shaped life differently in our dimension than in yours."

Andrew replied, "Yeah. How do you know that?"

"Basic Gerousian Physics," Matthew said, still taking notes from the POD's panels.

Andrew needed clarification. "Who?" he asked.

Matthew sighed and put down the pen and paper. He

rubbed his eyes and said, "Helmut Gerouse, the famous German physicist who explored relativity and time travel. Don't you know about him in your dimension?"

Andrew replied, "Sorry. Our person was named Einstein."

Matthew's eyebrows lifted high in surprise. "Albert Einstein?"

"Yeah! You've heard of him?" Andrew asked.

Matthew shook his head in disgust this time. "Yeah. He was committed to life in prison for trying unspeakable experiments on the general population. He attempted to send an entire city through time. The inhabitants of the city came back completely deformed or dead. It was a great tragedy."

"Our times have incredible differences. Your people are so different," Andy noted.

"Not any different than yours are to us," Matthew said. "And your people are really sad. Maybe you should consider spending some time here and learning a little more."

"Maybe after I've learned how to control this thing first. Right now, I just want to get home." And he truly did.

"Okay," Matthew said, "Well, let's go over what brought you here. Let me see your travel log and technical notes."

Andrew turned red, "Uh, you know, it's a funny thing about that. I don't exactly have…"

"You've got to be kidding me," Matthew sighed. "You aren't so different from your counterpart as you would like to think. Let's see what you've got going on here."

Matthew and Andrew went over the readings that Matthew wrote down. Andrew explained what he did, and Matthew explained very technical things to a confused but eager-to-learn Andrew.

After a while, Julie walked over to the POD. "So, Matthew, my friend. Can you fix this?"

Matthew ran his fingers through his hair. Julie leaned on his shoulder and ran her fingers through his hair as well, looking lovingly at him. Andrew felt the pangs of jealousy forming in the pit of his stomach but reminded himself that this was not his Julie. "I'm not sure. I think so. It's a real mess, and Andy here is so disorganized that I can't believe he made it here in one piece. It makes me nervous to think about what Andy has been up to and where he is now."

Julie glared at Andrew. "Just get him home and bring my Andy back. I don't care how many pieces this clown ends up in when he gets home. I want my husband back. I don't want to be stuck with some creepy look-alike for the rest of my life. I'd have to have him euthanized or shipped off to some other country."

Matthew replied, "The only problem with that is if he ends up in 22 pieces, your Andy will too."

Julie stared at Matthew. There was a hint of excess wetness in this woman's eyes. "Then get him home in one piece. Just get him home. This person may look like the man I fell in love with, but he's nowhere near to being that man. I want my man back, and looking at this copy hurts me too much. He's not the person I fell in love with. I wouldn't know how to have sex with any others without him."

"I only have one small concern, though," Matthew said softly.

"And that is?" Julie looked tired.

Matthew hesitated, "Whether or not I can direct him back to his own dimension. There are thousands, you know.

It's like trying to throw a needle and hit the sun."

"You mean like looking for a needle in a haystack?" Andrew said.

Matthew looked at him. "Why would anyone put a needle in a haystack?"

Andrew replied, "Why would anyone try throwing a needle at the sun?"

Matthew thought for a moment, "Touché. You know, you're not such a bad guy. I wouldn't mind getting to know you better."

"Likewise. But I'm eager to get home, so let's try it." Andrew said.

Julie threw up her hands, "For the love of God, kiss, make out, or whatever you two are going to do, but just get on with it and get him the hell out of here!" Then to Andrew, "No offense, but I hope I never see you again!"

Andrew looked at Julie and said, "Same to you, and no offense either."

The two offered cursory smiles at each other, knowing that, regardless of their differences, they still had a bond. Julie walked off into the house and slammed the door.

"I thought for a moment that we connected, but I'm not sure how sincere she was," Andrew told Mathew.

"You know, she's in there crying her eyes out," Matthew said. "Once we get her husband back, he and I will console her. Susie will come over and be there for her as well. A few weeks from now, a series of funny stories will end with the idea that this must never happen again."

"And I'll go back to my Julie and tell her about this place, and we'll both marvel at how an entire society can live this way."

Matthew asked, "Do you think your Julie will be suspicious about what might have happened while you were here? You know she'll have questions. She might speculate about what could have happened. You talked about jealousy, so I imagine her thoughts will have a tinge of that."

"Maybe," Andrew said thoughtfully.

"Don't take this the wrong way, Andy, but I feel sorry for you. I'm sure you'll be fine, but there will be times of tension. I hope you and your Julie can weather what's to come from this."

"Ours is a strong relationship," Andrew said. But deep inside, he wondered if he should even bring up this dimension. He would decide that when the time came.

Matthew worked on the computer in the POD, making calculations. He ran home and came back with books, notes, and tablets to look up more information. After a while, he poked his head out of the POD and said to Andrew, "I think it's ready."

Andrew looked up and smiled. "Tell me what you want me to do."

Matthew squeezed himself and Andrew into the POD. He explained the procedure and told Andrew what he could do on the off chance that he didn't end up in his dimension. Andrew was a little more than worried, but he trusted that Matthew knew what he was talking about.

"Okay. Just remember what I told you. This time, don't gun it," Matthew advised.

Andrew laughed, "Yeah. I'll ease it into drive."

"Good luck," Matthew said. He gave Andrew a hug and felt the warmth of affection in return. Matthew held him at arm's length. "I don't know how you feel about this in your dimension," Matthew said, "but I've known Andy all my life, and I don't think you'll mind." He kissed Andrew on the cheek. Oddly enough, at least in Andrew's mind, he didn't feel offended by the gesture but couldn't find it in him to return the kiss.

"I didn't mind at all," Andrew said. "I appreciate how close you and your Andrew are, and I know that you're doing this to get your friend back more than you are doing it to get rid of me."

"A friend is a friend," Matthew said. "Friendship knows no boundaries, whether by a distance of miles, time, or dimensions. You might not be the Andy of my world, but you're still my friend." Julie walked out of the house. Her eyes were red, and tear tracks stained her face. She looked at Matthew. "Well?" she asked.

"We're about to give it a try," Matthew said.

She looked at Andrew and said, "I can't say it's been fun, and I can't tell you I'll miss you. Don't ever come back here looking like my husband again. Just get the hell out of here. If you happen to see my husband, my sweet Andy, on your way back, please tell him I missed him even though it's only been a few hours. Will you do that?"

"If I happen to see him, I will tell him."

"Thanks," Julie said. "Now get inside and send him home to me." After saying the words, she chuckled and looked at Matthew. "I never thought I'd hear myself telling Andy, or anyone else, to get into the POD and get going." Matthew laughed, put his arm around Julie, and nodded to Andrew.

Andrew smiled, walked into the POD, and closed the door. He adjusted the controls as they had discussed, flipped the switch on the black box, and moved the lever a little at a time. Andrew felt his balance leave his head. He felt like he was splintering into a million pieces and then suddenly whole again. He slowly opened the door and peered out into the dim light.

"Did you forget something?" Julie asked, taking the camera down from her face.

"What?" Andrew was still confused by his ordeal.

"Well, you just walked in, shut the door, and then did your 'creepy face sticking out the door' look. Aren't you going to try it?"

Andrew opened the door all the way and stepped out of the POD. He walked over to Julie and looked at her. He marveled that moments ago, he was saying goodbye to a woman who looked exactly like her but acted so differently.

"Andrew," Julie broke the awkward silence, "is everything okay?"

"What did you call me?" he asked.

"Andrew. I called you Andrew. Should I be calling you something else?" Julie was becoming a little concerned.

"No, no. That's perfect." He grabbed Julie and hugged her, almost causing her to drop the camera.

"Maybe I should have you stand in the POD more often," Julie said, smiling to herself.

"I have an amazing story to tell you," Andrew said. "Let's go into the house and sit down." Andrew put his arm around her, and they walked into the house. He loved feeling Julie by his side.

"Mr. B?"

Andrew turned to see Kota standing quietly by the POD.

"Does this mean I must wait for my turn to float again?"

"I'm so sorry, Kota. Let's do that tomorrow, please. I've just had an interesting adventure. Let me tell Julie about it, and maybe we can tell you some of it tomorrow. And then you can float. Deal?"

"Yeah. Deal." Kota pouted. Then she brightened up. "What time?"

"Right after breakfast. Ten o'clock."

CHAPTER 12

Not as Far as You Think

When we expect something, our minds can convince us that we have achieved it even if, in reality, that is not the case. The reverse can also be true. If someone blindfolded you and put a piece of chocolate in your mouth, it would take time to figure out what it is, especially if you've been told it was something different. I'm saying that our senses can be deceived, and our minds can play along. It becomes difficult to discern what reality is and isn't, even when reality is staring you right in the face and laughing at you.~ Andrew Barton

"This weekend," Andrew said to himself, "no heading off into other dimensions, timelines, or anyplace where I might find myself or anyone I think I know. I think. I hope!" After last weekend, Andrew was almost ready to give in and give up, but something continued to drive him. Julie wasn't sure what to think about his story of another Julie. She thought he sounded sincere but had to wonder if he blacked out for a moment and dreamt the entire thing. "Blacked out?" he said. "I know what I saw and heard and felt. I just returned at the exact time that I left in our time." What he didn't know was that she had doubts. Suppose he was telling the truth, and it did happen as he said it did. In that case, another woman was running around doing things she had only dreamt about but would never do or even admit to in this world or this life. She had to wonder if Andrew was still happy with his life.

"What are you doing today?" Julie had appeared from nowhere, startling Andrew in his thoughts.

"Well," he started, "I'm making a few adjustments to the POD structure to see if it will travel into space."

"Space?" Julie questioned and then chuckled. "Certainly, you don't mean outer space, do you?" She was afraid that his answer would confirm her fears, and it did.

"Of course, outer space. What other kind of space is there?" Andrew said, smiling at the thought that there might be some other kind that he would travel to.

Julie sighed. "Andrew, I know you've probably already thought this out, but please tell me how you will do that for my sake, the sake of our child, and my sanity. You have no space suit, helmet, or oxygen tanks. How will this work?"

Andrew looked at Julie with mild surprise. "Do you remember a few weekends ago when I ended up in another dimension with everyone who looked like us but wasn't us?"

"I remember that," she said to Andrew with a slight sour taste in her mouth.

"Do you remember how you thought I hadn't even left, and yet I spent hours in that alternate dimension?"

"I remember that, Andrew. What's your point?" Julie didn't want to talk about the other dimension. Her greatest desire was discovering how Andrew intended to get about in space without suffocating.

"In our time, no time had passed," Andrew started, "which means that in our time, my trip would be instantaneous, so I wouldn't need oxygen for an instantaneous trip." Andrew was proud of his logic.

Julie, on the other hand, could see no logic in this. She was beginning to wonder if something had happened to Andrew on this last trip away from home that had hurt his good sense. "I can see what you're saying, Andrew," she started, "but here's my concern. You'll take off and be back here in what will seem like no time at all to me. Is that correct?"

Andrew nodded his head.

Julie continued, "But you might be gone several hours or even days, right? And if there had been poisoned air in that other dimension you visited, do you believe you could have breathed naturally just as you are now?"

Again, Andrew nodded, then shook his head. As if Julie had hit him over the head with a plank, he realized the implications of what she was asking: "I need to seal this up airtight and get an oxygen source."

Julie smiled but was still worried about Andrew. Why didn't he see this before? What was going on in his mind? Was this even 'her' Andrew?

Julie smiled at Andrew and said, "Keep working on this, and we can discuss it again later." She turned and walked into the house.

She heard knocking at the front door. When she answered it, Matt was smiling broadly.

"Hey, Julie!" He said. "Is your hubby around?"

"Well, my dear friend," Julie said, "where would you look if you were trying to find him?"

Matt thought momentarily, then said, "In the garage?"

Julie wagged her finger at him and said, "Oh, you scoundrel. You figured it out!"

Matt scowled. "What's going on, Julie?"

"I'm sorry, Matt. I'm concerned about Andrew. Earlier, he was talking about taking the POD into space but didn't even stop to consider he needed oxygen. He's been distracted. He's not thinking right. Matt, I'm afraid he might not be the Andrew I married. I wouldn't even know how to ask."

"I don't know how much I can help," Matt said, "but I'm happy to keep an eye on him and ensure he doesn't hurt himself. I've known him for a long time, Julie, and I'll know if it's not him. Do you mind if I head to the garage and begin my undercover work?"

Julie smiled. "Go get him, Matt. And thank you!"

Matt walked out to the garage. "Hey, buddy!" Matt laughed and slapped Andrew on the back.

"Hi, Matt," Andrew said, smiling. "What brings you over today?"

"Uh," Matt stopped and looked at Andrew, confused. "You!" he said.

"What do you mean?" Andrew asked.

"You asked me to come by," Matt continued. "Don't you remember calling me around nine o'friggin clock this morning? You knew I was out late last night, and still, you called me up with my head echoing every electronic gong on my cell and begged me to come by today to help with some trip you wanted to try out with the POD."

Andrew thought hard, and it reflected on his face.

"Hmm. Nope," he said, sighing, "I don't remember doing that."

Matt thought sure that he was ready to strangle his good friend when Andrew broke out into a huge smile and burst out laughing.

"I'm sorry, Matt," Andrew gasped between his short outbursts of laughter. "I couldn't help myself." He wiped a tear from his eye and put his hands on Matt's shoulders. "I'm sorry, my friend. I didn't mean to make your hangover worse than it is. I really wanted you to be a part of this."

Now, it was Matt's turn to stare. Momentarily, though, he had forgotten about the pain in his head and the sick feeling in his stomach. For one brief moment, he felt numb. Now, it all started to return a bit more than before it left. "If I didn't like you so much," Matt said, "I'd throw up either on your shoes or inside your POD thing. Either scenario would teach you a lesson, but I'd settle for an Alka Seltzer and some Advil at this point. Then you can explain more to me what you're talking about." Matt sat down on the garage floor. The cool concrete felt good, and he wanted to lay his head down on it, but he knew he would either hit his head too hard or fall asleep. Either choice wasn't good.

Andrew ran into the house to fulfill Matt's request. He stood over his friend with a glass of bubbling, transparent liquid and some round red pills. "Here ya go, buddy," Andrew said, "I'm sorry you aren't feeling well. I can just do this by myself if you want." Andrew was sincere.

Matt looked up at his friend. His head continued to throb, and his eyes hurt.

"It's okay. I'll be fine. I don't want to miss out on whatever this is you want to share. And it'll all be good if I don't throw up somewhere in the middle of it."

"You're welcome to just wait here, and I'll fill you in when I get back."

"No," Matt said, struggling to his feet. "I'll go with you and give you a hand."

"Are you sure?" Andrew asked. He seemed very concerned now.

"Nah, and thanks for the meds," Matt said. "I'm already feeling better." He walked over to the POD, put his hand against it, struck a Bogart pose, and said, "So, where we taking this thing schweetheart?"

"Funny, Bogie. We're going into space."

Matt looked at the POD he was leaning against. "In this thing?"

"Yeah, why not?" Andrew almost looked hurt.

"I hate to be the one to break this to you, but there are a few things you need to think about. First of all, this thing isn't airtight." Matt actually felt smarter than Andrew for a moment.

"So?" Andrew shrugged.

"So!?" Matt was once again appalled at what he heard. "So, just that when you get into the vacuum of space, and your insides get pulled out and spread from here to Jupiter, and your POD floats away to the deep, dark, cold recesses of space, you'll be doing it alone because I'm not getting in that thing until you make it space worthy."

Andrew stared at him. "You're crazy."

"I'm crazy? I used to think that you were smart and sane. I looked up to you, and now you're acting like some kind of lunatic!" Matt leaned his back against the POD door. "You're not getting back into this thing. Not until you agree to do some things to make it a little safer.”

Andrew’s face twisted into an evil version of the kind man he always portrayed. His voice deepened, and when he spoke, the growl from his throat wasn’t friendly. “Get out of the way, Matt.”

“Holy crap! Who the heck are you?” Matt’s eyes grew wide.

“Don’t make me have to move you,” Andrew threatened.

Matt stood his ground. He was a championship wrestler in high school and knew that, if he needed to, he could take Andrew down and hold him for a while at least. As he prepared himself for Andrew’s charge, he overlooked the shuttering of the POD behind him and the slight hum and shimmer that accompanied it. Andrew took a step toward Matt as the door behind Matt began to open. The pressure on his back made him instinctively push back. The door pushed harder, and a familiar voice sounded from the small crack that was forming.

“Hey! Who put something in front of the door? Hello? A little help here!”

The voice belonged to Andrew. Matt took a small step forward, allowing the door to open slightly more. In the meantime, Andrew, in front of Matt, stopped in his tracks, staring at the door. “Don’t open it!” Andrew yelled at Matt. “It’s a trick. It’s Andrew from another dimension. He’s here to destroy the POD!” Andrew lunged at Matt, taking him off balance.

Matt quickly grabbed Andrew and rolled to the floor with him. He caught a movement above him and looked up. Andrew stepped out of the POD. Another Andrew.

"Matt?" the other Andrew said. "What are you doing? Why are you wrestling in my garage?" He stared for a moment. "And, who are you wrestling?"

Matt looked up and lost his focus for a moment. When he did, the Andrew he was fighting pushed him off of him and jumped to his feet. He looked at Andrew standing at the POD door. "I'll be back." He pushed a button on his belt, shimmered, and vanished.

The garage was quiet, except for Matt, breathing heavily while sitting on the garage floor. He looked up at the POD doorway where Andrew was still standing. Andrew was shocked. He didn't know what to say and continued to stare at the spot from where the other Andrew had vanished. "I liked our lives when we were in high school," Matt said. "At least when we had someone to deal with, it was someone that we could deal with! Not someone that started a fight then vanished into thin air!" The room remained silent. "Are you going to say anything?"

Andrew swallowed. He blinked. "I'm not sure what to say," he said quietly. "I don't even know who that was or why he was here. It was me, but it wasn't me."

"It wasn't you," Matt huffed. "He wasn't anything like you. Well, he looked like you. He dressed like you. So, he looked and dressed like you but didn't act like you. So, I guess that even though he wasn't you, he was a you look alike, bent on taking over the world and making all creatures subject to his evil rule."

"What?" Andrew looked at Matt for the first time since the stranger vanished. Matt was grinning from ear to ear and still huffing and puffing.

"I had to get your attention somehow, buddy!" Matt

stood up and walked over to the POD. "Don't worry about that guy," he said. "We'll take care of him. Just let him try to come back. We know who he is now!"

"And just who is he?" Andrew smiled and waited for the reply.

"The other, weird you. You know, the maniacal Andrew. He'll be easy to spot by the," Matt stopped and thought for a moment, "by the maniacal things that he does."

Andrew laughed out loud. "You're the best, buddy." Andrew stepped down out of the POD and gave Matt a big hug.

"Whoa! Whoa!" Matt broke the hold and backed up. "What's with the hugging? We don't...hug." Then Matt squinted his eyes at Andrew and asked, "Who are you?" Then he started to laugh. "Ha. Got you. You thought I was serious."

"Yeah, Matt," Andrew chuckled, "you had me going there for a bit. But now we must figure out where he came from and how to prevent him from returning. What were his true intentions anyway?"

Matt looked at Andrew. "Nothing, really. He just wanted to take the POD into space that's all."

"What!" Andrew yelled. "He wanted to take it where? How could he even think about that? It's not ready. It's not airtight, and there's no oxygen supply. He would have…" Andrew stopped in mid-sentence. He thought for a moment and began pacing. "He would have pushed that button on his belt and gone home or wherever he's from. The POD would have been destroyed, and everyone would have assumed that I had been as well. Good thing he didn't realize I was inside working. Or maybe he did!"

CHAPTER 13

France

"Yeah." Matt said nonchalantly, asking, "When did you go in there, anyway?"

"I had been in there for about half an hour, I guess," Andrew said. "I took it on a spin through time and distance, but here on Earth. To everyone here, when I leave and come back, it's like I haven't left at all since I can return at the exact moment I leave. When I got back, I was making a few adjustments inside. Then I heard thumping against the door and tried to come out. You know the rest."

"I do?" Matt questioned. "The rest of what?"

"The rest of the story," Andrew said.

"What story?" Matt asked. But when Andrew gave him a scolding look, Matt took a deep breath and said, "Oh yeah! That story. Sorry. I'm a little slow and hung over today."

"I asked you last night to come by," Andrew said, turning back toward the POD, "you shouldn't have gone out drinking."

"You called me this morning," Matt said.

Andrew looked over his shoulder. "To remind you, but I called you last night to invite you. That's when you said you would love to, or something like that."

"Oh yeah. And I was excited about this, but then Susie said she'd go out with me, and, honestly, I think we had a perfect time. I can't help it if we were a little carried away," Matt said.

"It's still no reason to..." Andrew stopped and stared at Matt. "Did you say that Susie went out with you?"

"Yeah. Finally!" Matt said, grinning like a Cheshire cat. "I couldn't believe it myself. I thought it was the weirdest thing ever. I asked her, like I always do, you know, jokingly, and she said yes! And it was a great date. I think we'll be going out again, maybe next week."

Andrew was inwardly concerned but figured he'd talk to Julie or Susie about it later. Still, something didn't seem right about the whole situation. "That's great, buddy," Andrew said as upbeat as possible. "So, are you feeling up to taking a little trip with me in this thing?" Andrew patted the POD like it was a vintage car.

"Not into space, right?" Matt said cautiously.

Andrew laughed, "No, silly. I already told you that I would never do that. At least not until it's properly prepared and ready to go. I was thinking that we could go to the French countryside."

Matt smiled, waiting for Andrew to say something about joking. But Matt knew he was serious. "This thing can go to France?"

"This 'thing,' as you call it, can go anywhere that there are magnetic lines of force." Andrew opened the door and stepped up into the opening. "Are you coming?" he asked

Matt.

"How long will we be gone?" Matt asked.

"Only about 10 minutes tops," Andrew replied. "Why? Got a hot date this morning?" Andrew smiled and turned to go back inside the POD.

"No," Matt said, sounding like a hurt little kid. "I'm comin'," he said, stepping inside with Andrew.

Andrew reached over and closed the door, latching it with a large circular device.

"Is this a submarine now," Matt asked. "It looks like what they show on TV on the submarine doors."

"It's an efficient way of sealing a door tightly," Andrew said, turning the wheel one more time.

Matt looked around at the inside of the POD. "Wow, buddy. You've really spruced this thing up. Two seats now?"

"Only the best for the people I love," Andrew said.

"Can I sit over there," Matt asked, pointing to the seat next to a control console.

"Mmm, no," Andrew said, sitting quickly in the seat. "That's for the pilot. Maybe someday I'll teach you how to fly this machine, but not today."

Matt stretched out his arms and realized he couldn't touch the walls. "Did you make this thing bigger?" He asked Andrew.

"No. I just moved things around for efficiency. Makes it look bigger. Someday, I'll make it bigger, but not today."

Matt shrugged it off and watched the flashing lights and computer screens as maps and symbols appeared.

The entire POD began to hum. "Are you ready?" Andrew asked Matt excitedly.

"Yeah," Matt said, starting to feel somewhat nervous.

"I guess."

"Then," Andrew grinned wider than Matt had ever seen, "hold on!"

With that, Matt held on to the seat as tightly as possible. He closed his eyes and wished for a moment that he hadn't agreed to do this. He felt light-headed for a second, and then there was nothing.

"You can open your eyes now," Andrew said. "We're here."

Matt slowly opened one eye and then the other. He was still holding tightly to the seat of his chair and, realizing this, carefully released his grip. "We're here?"

"Uh huh," Andrew said, smiling.

"Cool. When can we get out? I'd love to see the outside. The daylight and the beach. I want to smell the salt air." He had never been claustrophobic before but didn't feel as comfortable as he wanted inside the POD.

"We can get out right now!" Andrew said. "We should be right by the ocean." Andrew turned the wheel and opened the door.

The rush of hot and humid air surprised both Andrew and Matt. Andrew had expected the humidity but not the blast of heat! Light, brighter than the inside of the POD, streamed in through the door, but it wasn't as bright as Andrew thought it should be. He looked outside, and his heart sank. Instead of seeing the beach with its ocean and waves, he saw a jungle. The loud sound of insects surrounded him, and a hot breeze blew in the door.

"I don't want to be a backseat driver," Matt said, "but I think you might have taken a wrong turn somewhere around England. This really doesn't look like the coast of France."

"It's got to be right," Andrew said. "I'm sure that I set the coordinates correctly."

Andrew returned to the center of the POD and looked at the readings on various panels and screens. "According to everything I can see, we should be where I wanted us to be. The GPS isn't working, which bothers me a little." Andrew turned back toward the door, but Matt was no longer there. "Matt!" he yelled.

"What?" The reply echoed in from the outside.

Andrew ran to the door and looked out. Matt was outside looking at some strange plants near the POD. "Matt! What are you doing?"

"I've never seen anything like this, Andrew. Have you?" Matt pointed to the plant. A giant bulb at the top of a long stem was beginning to open, and long reddish-purple strands were finding their way out into the humid air.

Andrew squinted to see what Matt was looking at. "No, I haven't ever seen a plant like that. I wouldn't get too close to it until we figure out what it is."

"Ah, come on. I've never seen a plant I couldn't handle," Matt said, "except maybe poison ivy. But then, it's not meant to be handled. You know what I mean, buddy?"

"Yes, Matt. I know what you mean. Why don't you come back inside until I figure out what happened?"

"It's nice to stretch my legs after that long trip," Matt said.

"Long trip? We were only in the POD for three minutes," Andrew exclaimed.

"Yeah, but we came a long way. At least this doesn't look anything like where we were when we left."

"Maybe that's it," Andrew mumbled to himself and

turned back toward the panels inside. He entered a few numbers into the computer and was shocked to see the result. "I figured it out, Matt!" Andrew yelled. "We didn't go far from our location at all distance-wise. We're actually in the same spot where we started. We're just way farther back in time!"

Andrew turned back toward the door. "Matt?" he yelled. Andrew looked out of the doorway, but Matt was nowhere to be found. "Matt!" he yelled again and listened. The only thing he could hear was the loud buzzing of the insects.

Andrew's frustration was reaching a new level. He couldn't just leave his friend here but also didn't want to leave the POD alone. In his mind, however, he had no choice. He had to find Matt. He wished that he had built a door he could lock from the outside, but he never foresaw the need for one. Andrew made a mental note to take care of that when he returned home. He stepped out into the damp heat of the day and closed the door behind him. Then, he realized he had no idea which way to go. There were nothing but trees and ground plants all around him. He looked to see if any of the plants had been disturbed and saw what he thought was a slight trampling of the grass off to the left.

"I wish I had been a better Boy Scout," he said to himself. He slowly started to walk in the direction he thought Matt had gone. This jungle was creepy, and he wasn't sure exactly how far back in time he went. What creatures were around? Was something going to jump out and have him for a midday snack?

Andrew tried to clear his mind of unpleasant thoughts and only focused on finding Matt. Why would he wander off like that? Andrew took another step, not looking where he was going when the ground suddenly gave way under his feet. He fell down through the ground, falling rapidly. No, he wasn't falling as much as he was sliding. He stopped with a thud at the bottom of the slide and checked to make sure he was okay. "At least I'm not hurt," he said. He noticed there was light. He was underground, and yet light came from somewhere. The walls seemed to glow softly, but the combined soft glow of the ceiling, walls, and floor gave the illusion of constant bright light.

He looked at the slide that had brought him to this place and tried to climb back up, but it was too slippery, and his attempts simply resulted in him ending up at the bottom again. "Well, Andrew," he said to himself, "it looks like you have no choice but to follow the yellow brick road and hope that you find Matt the scarecrow at the end."

He walked for what seemed like an hour before he reached a door. The door was made of metal and was partially opened. "Weird to find a metal door underground," he said out loud. "I really wonder what's going on?" He pushed the door open more and peered around to find yet another long corridor. Although this one still had the lighted surfaces, it looked more to be the part of a building. "Stranger and stranger," he said to himself and continued walking toward whatever awaited him at the end.

He started to feel chilled and realized his clothes were still slightly damp from the humidity from above, and then he realized that it wasn't humid down here, nor was it hot. In fact, it was pretty chilly. As he continued to walk, he could swear that he could feel a breeze blowing on him. He held up his hand to feel where the breeze might be coming from and followed it to what appeared to be a hidden air vent. It wasn't so much hidden as it was disguised. There was some type of image over the front of it. It was a light image that looked solid and three-dimensional, but when Andrew reached up to touch it, his hand passed through it, and he could feel the grate. He wasn't sure how he noticed the grate, but something was off about that particular spot. It wasn't a part of the wall, and as good as the false light cover was, it still did not look quite right. "Who created all of this?" Andrew wondered out loud.

He heard a noise from farther down the hallway. A distinct click, almost like a door closing quietly. He started walking down the hallway again, but more slowly this time. The hallway curved around to the right, and Andrew followed cautiously. He couldn't see around the corner and wondered if someone was there. As he rounded the corner, he saw that the hallway ended, and three doors were at the end. They were the same style of metal doors that he had seen when he first entered the hallway. One was at the very end of the hall. As he faced it, there was another door to his left and one to his right. He wasn't sure which one to try first.

He walked up to the center door and put his ear against it. There was no sound that he could hear. He moved to the one on his right and again listened. He could hear muffled talking. Andrew wasn't sure what was being said, but at first, he thought he heard arguing. Then he realized that it was not arguing, just a conversation he couldn't understand. Then he heard the laugh. It was Matt's laugh. He turned the knob slowly and started to push the door open when it suddenly gave way and opened quickly on its own.

CHAPTER 14

The Governor

Andrew fell into the room and almost hit the ground, but he managed to catch himself. He stood, dumbfounded by what he saw. Several people were in this large room sitting at tables. Most of them were dressed in the same uniform. The uniforms were gray and white, with a black stripe down the pants' leg and a symbol on the upper right chest of the shirts. The symbol looked very familiar. It was made up of three solid black circles.

Looking around the room at everyone staring at him, he saw Matt sitting at a table not too far from the door. Matt waved wildly at Andrew with his free hand, which didn't have the fried chicken leg.

"Andrew! Over here!" he shouted. Then he turned to the people at the table with him and said, "This is him! This is the guy I was telling you about!" Everyone stood up and began to applaud.

Andrew was as confused as he had ever been. He was stunned and couldn't move. Finally, Matt got up from the table amidst the cheering and clapping. He helped his friend up and escorted Andrew back to his table.

Matt pulled out a chair for Andrew and, placing his hands on Andrew's shoulders, gently pushed him down into the seat!

Andrew looked around the table at the people who sat silently, staring and smiling shyly at Andrew. He smiled weakly at one person who was looking intently at him. As soon as Andrew smiled, the person turned red and looked away. Andrew was about to ask Matt what was going on when a person that Andrew could only think of as a waiter came over and hovered over Andrew's chair. Andrew looked up and, again, smiled weakly. The waiter almost passed out from excitement, and once he regained his composure, he cleared his throat.

"Hello, Mr. Barton," the waiter said. "Let me just say it's an extreme honor to meet you and bring you your meal tonight. Oh my goodness, I can't believe I'm the first to talk to you! My friends will never believe it. I hope you'll allow me to get a photo with you later tonight."

"Uh, sure," Andrew said.

"What can I get you, Mr. Barton? Anything you want, and it's all on the house!"

"Oh, uh, thank you so much," Andrew stammered.

He looked at Matt, who was eating again. Matt held up the chicken leg and said, "Oh buddy, you've got to try this. It has got to be the best chicken dinner I've ever had. Amazing!"

Andrew watched Matt devour the chicken and was shocked to see another waiter run over and put more chicken on his plate.

Andrew looked at his waiter and said, "I'll just have what he's having," and pointed to Matt's plate.

"Oh, perfect! Excellent, sir. I'll have that out to you immediately. And if it's not cooked to your liking, just let me know, and I'll ensure it's taken care of right away!" The waiter backed away slowly. Andrew thought he was going to bow out of the room, but instead, he glanced over at another waiter and mouthed, "I'm serving Andrew Barton!"

Andrew turned back to Matt. He was about to ask, again, what was going on when he noticed that everyone else at the table continued to stare at him and didn't touch their food. "You all really should eat before your meals get cold," Andrew told them. They all immediately picked up their forks and started eating, only taking their eyes off Andrew to see what they were picking up to put in their mouths.

Matt leaned over and nudged Andrew. "Pretty cool, eh?"

"What is going on?" Andrew asked.

"Well, apparently, you were wrong about where we were and even more wrong about when we were or are."

"Oh?" Andrew sat back a little and raised his eyebrows.

"And you know this how?"

"I asked," Matt shrugged. He took another bite of chicken and sat quietly.

After being unable to stand it any longer, Andrew asked, "So where and when are we?"

"Oh yeah," Matt said, swallowing his bite. "Well, we're not in the past. We're in the future. Way far in the future. It's pretty cool. And we're not that far from the house either, or where it used to be when you lived in it. Anyway, it seems that you come up with some pretty cool stuff during your lifetime, and somebody writes a book about you called The Weekend Adventures of Andrew Barton or something like that. Turns out that there's a whole bunch of them. Books, that is. And they talk about you and your experiments, me, Susie, Julie, and everyone. So here in this time period, we're like celebrities or something. They knew we were coming and have been expecting us."

Matt took a gulp of what looked like a soda. He took a breath and then finished the glass. "This is so cool," Matt told Andrew. "Cola has come a long way since our time. Watch this."

Matt picked up a pitcher of water and his empty glass. "You tell the glass what you want, and it makes it." He looked at the glass and said, "Cherry Cola." He started pouring the clear water from the pitcher into the glass, and it turned into a dark reddish, caramel-colored liquid. "It even fizzes and is cold!" Matt took a sip. "You should try it."

"Wait a minute," Andrew said, putting his hands up to stop the barrage of words from leaving Matt's mouth. "How did you get down here? Let's start with that."

"Oh, that's an easy one. I know this," Matt said, drinking more soda. "When I walked out of the POD, I went a little ways behind it, and this guy came running up to me and told me that I couldn't be there, and he started to escort me to some security office. He takes out this really cool-looking tablet thing and starts to talk to it, then asks me my name. I told him, and he took a picture, and then we stopped. He got all excited, and the next thing I knew, I was at this banquet. They sent someone back to get you, but you had disappeared."

"Wait a minute. Security office? Is this some kind of military base or something?"

Matt laughed and tried to keep from spitting out his pop. "Military? The farthest thing from it, my friend. This is the Rocky Mountain Disneyland. Crazy huh? Who would have guessed we'd have a theme park just down the road from us?"

"So, where did we land?" Andrew almost sounded disappointed.

"That's the best part! We landed in Dinosaurland."

The waiter brought Andrew his meal and hovered over him, watching him take his first bite. Andrew was about to tell the waiter how good the meal was but was interrupted by a small commotion in the hallway outside another door. The door flew open, and several people with lights on their heads and lenses on either side came crowding in, lining the other side of the room. Once they were all in, a very regal-looking woman entered amidst the Ooo's and Ahhh's of the other people eating. The regal woman floated over to Andrew and looked down at him. "Are you Andrew Barton?" she asked.

"Yes, ma'am," he said and somehow felt the need to stand up.

The regal woman stuck out her hand and shook Andrew's. "I'm Governor Sorenson. I was notified of your unusual arrival and canceled my afternoon plans so that I could meet with you."

"Oh, uh, wonderful," Andrew said, glancing down at his food.

"Please, finish your meal. We can chat here for a little while. Then, when you've finished, I can show you and Matthew how things have changed."

Matt stuck out his hand around Andrew. "Matt Berman. Nice to meet you. I'm not usually into politics, but I'll make an exception for you."

The Governor laughed. "Your sense of humor is exactly how it's described in the books."

Matt wasn't sure if that was good or bad, so he kept quiet for a while.

Andrew sat back down and picked at his food. The Governor sat across from him at the table, causing employees to scamper to other seats. Every now and again, the Governor would smile at a person or two standing by the walls with their strange headsets in place. Andrew assumed that they were press.

"Mr. Barton," the Governor began, "this is a momentous occasion for us. We had read how you would come to visit us, but we had no idea when that time would occur. I'm very happy that it happened during my term as Governor." The Governor spoke the last few words a little louder than the rest and turned to smile at the media reporters. Several employees applauded.

"I'm afraid you have the advantage then," Andrew said between bites. "I had no idea that we were coming here today, but it will be nice to be able to talk with you about my future."

The room became quiet, and Andrew wondered what he had said. He was about to find out.

The Governor looked very sternly at Andrew. "Your future, Mr. Barton, is something that we will not discuss while you are here. In fact, we will not discuss anything with the word 'future' in it again from this time until you leave. Is that clear?"

Andrew had stopped chewing but swallowed at the Governor's final word. "Yes, ma'am."

The Governor smiled and sat back in her chair again. "There is so much to tell you about how this part of the country has changed and so much to show you before you leave. Before we go for our tour, however, do you have any general questions for me?"

All Andrew could think of was the one thing he was told he couldn't discuss. His future. So he tried hard to think of something else. "So I assume that I am known to you for my ability to travel through time," he said proudly.

The Governor chuckled. "Actually, Mr. Barton, your time travel exploits are one of the least things you are known for as you never shared that ability with the rest of the world. The major contribution you made to the world was your magnetic propulsion drive. It's not only used to power vehicles here on Earth, but we use it on all of our spacecraft. The use of the magnetic drive has even reached other galaxies thanks to one of your descendants who traveled to a distant planet known as Khizara. Oh yes, Mr. Barton, your magnetic drive created quite a future. But let's walk so I can show you how much this city has changed. I think that you'll be impressed with how the future has developed. Besides, it's becoming quite stuffy in here with all these people, don't you think?"

Andrew took a final bite of his chicken and stood from the table. Matt stood with him. When the Governor stood, she maneuvered herself between Matt and Andrew, put her arms around them and smiled for the cameras, turning this way and that until she was tired of smiling. Being the grand politician she was, however, she gently guided her guests to the door and up the stairs. Andrew was shocked to see the large gift shop when they emerged from the well-hidden catacombs of twists and turns from their dining area to the top. Hundreds of people were crowded into the shop, waving cards around at what appeared to be a cashier. Shortly after they appeared, a rumble of low voices rippled through the shop, and camera devices began to flash again as the

Governor led her guests through the shop and to the door. As they pushed their way through the crowded room, Andrew thought he heard a woman's voice exclaim, "I touched him!" and the rumble of voices increased as the crowd shifted slightly to see the woman who touched the new guests.

When they were outside, there was a little more freedom to move around as a line of security guards surrounded the three dignitaries and moved with them. Andrew wondered how celebrities ever got used to this and smiled at the fact that his fifteen minutes of fame happened long after he would be dead, but that he was here to see it!

The Governor showed Andrew and Matt around for two hours.

"Mr. Barton," The Governor said, "This is the Barton Museum. I thought you would be interested to see how we've recreated your garage working area and a few of your early inventions."

"This is amazing!" Andrew said as he looked around the museum. "It's almost as if you brought my garage here."

"Well, it's certainly not my doing," The Governor said. "Meet Gerrand Markell, the curator of this fine establishment.

"Oh, Mr. Barton," the shorter and slight man said, sticking out his hand. "It's such a joy to meet you! I've devoted my life to showing people the early years of Andrew Barton. I hope you'll approve, and please let me know if you see any inaccuracies so I can accurately show the world who you were or are. Oh my goodness, I'm so flustered," he said as he shook Andrew's hand.

"These displays are interesting. Where did you find this equipment?" Andrew asked.

"Oh, here and there," Garrand said, shrugging his shoulders. "Do you find them authentic?"

"For the most part," Andrew said.

Garrand furrowed his brow and grabbed what appeared to be a tablet without a screen. "Tell me how I can make these displays more authentic. I want the world to be transported back in time and feel like they're right there in the garage with you."

Andrew pointed out minor details here and there that needed changing. The museum curator eagerly wrote down those changes and thanked Andrew over and over for the information. As Matt and Andrew were getting ready to leave, much to the delight of a very bored Matt, the curator shook Andrew's hand again.

"You have been very helpful in helping us to accurately show people how you lived. All of this," he spread his arm and turned slowly, indicating the entire museum, "shows how you helped our society reach the level it has. Thank you for that. I also wanted to thank you for the gracious Gift that made our collection complete."

The Governor, waiting to walk out the door, suddenly turned and put her arm around Andrew's shoulders. "We need to hurry off now," she said, pulling Andrew toward the door.

Andrew resisted and asked the curator, "Gift? What Gift are you referring to?"

The curator glanced at the Governor. Andrew also looked to see that the Governor was giving the curator a very cross look.

"What gift?" Andrew insisted.

"Why, the original POD. We could never locate it, but we are very grateful since you brought it to us."

"Wait a second. There must be some mistake. I didn't bring the POD to you. I wasn't even planning on coming here; this was an accident, and I need to get back home. Come on, Matt. Let's get back to the POD."

"I'm afraid that your POD is no longer where you left it," the Governor said. "We've had it moved. I was hoping to tell you about this after you had been here a while and seen more of our world, but since the cat is out of the bag, I guess I'll have to insist that you stay. Please don't try anything heroic. Remember, we have the book of your life story and know how you try to get your POD back. Rest assured, Mr. Barton, that we will do everything possible to prevent you from retrieving it."

"But my family," Andrew said.

"Your family will just think that you left in the POD and vanished mysteriously one day. It's for the best, Mr. Barton. I'm sure that you'll enjoy living out the rest of your life here." The Governor motioned to two nearby security people who came over and stood beside both Matt and Andrew. "These gentlemen will show you to your residence. You'll have full access to our finest scientific facilities, Mr. Barton, where you can continue to tinker and invent at the cost of the state. You and Mr. Berman will want for nothing."

"I will want for my family," Andrew protested.

"Yeah, and I'll miss my friends at home," Matt said. "And I was just making progress with Susie, too," Matt sighed.

The security guards took Andrew and Matt away. The Governor motioned again, and another security guard brought her a book. She opened it up, watched as the words on page 119 changed, and rewrote themselves to reflect what had just happened. She closed the book and smiled. "You aren't the only one who can change history, Mr. Barton."

CHAPTER 15

Family

Andrew paced around the room. Matt watched the video wall.

"It's pretty cool," Matt said, lying on the sofa. "The oldies are episodes of things I haven't even seen yet! Oh, the things I'll tell our friends when we get home."

"Don't you mean if we get home?" Andrew asked.

"I have confidence in you, buddy," Matt said, flipping through channels. His hands danced in the air, pressing buttons on a panel that floated in front of Matt but was unseen to Andrew. Andrew found it a humorous distraction from the problem plaguing him. "I know you'll figure out something. You'll miss Julie and Stephanie too much. Your family means everything to you."

"I'm glad you're so confident, Matt. I just wish I could come up with an idea…Wait, what did you say?"

"What?" Matt said distractedly.

"What did you say about family?"

"That you would miss them. I'll miss them too come to think of it."

"That might be what helps us get back," Andrew said and walked to another wall.

"Missing them will get us back? I don't get it," Matt said, looking at Andrew.

Andrew walked up to the wall and said, "Display information on descendants of Andrew Barton in this geographical area." A wall section started to glow, and names and addresses appeared. "List direct descendants." Numerous names vanished, and two remained. Andrew reached up and pressed the contact button next to the first one. A sign came up stating that contact was being established.

A voice came from the wall. "Hello? Who's this?"

"Um," Andrew hadn't planned what to say. "This is Andrew Barton, and I was wondering if you were any relation..."

The wall suddenly lit up, and a girl in her mid-twenties appeared. Andrew took a step back and gasped.

Matt, who had been drawn back to the television, turned and stood up. "Buddy, how did you get a hold of Julie?"

Andrew didn't hear Matt but stepped back up toward the wall. "It's amazing!" he said.

"My name is Jolena," the girl said. "I heard you were here but never thought you'd try to contact me. You're my grandfather with many greats in front of it."

"And you are the spitting image of my wife," he said. "It's amazing what genetics do."

"Yeah, really," Jolena said. "Hey, do you want to get

together? We could talk about family stuff and the books written about you. Hey, who's that behind you? Is that Matt? He's cuter than described in the book."

Matt's ears perked up, and so did attention. He turned from the video wall and took a step toward Andrew. "Did someone say I'm cute?"

"Down, boy," Andrew said. "Do you have a copy of the book you're talking about? The one that describes Matt?"

"Sure," she said. "I have a copy of the original. It was like, your daughter that wrote it."

"How do we get to where you are?" Andrew asked.

"According to my V.I.D., you're not too far. Looks like you're in a hotel, so just go down to the lobby and tell the LobbyTech to get you a transxi, then tell the driver to bring you here." Jolena leaned forward and pushed something. A slip of paper spit out of the wall just below her image.

"Thank you, Jolena," Andrew said. "We'll be there as soon as possible if that's okay."

"Yeah, for sure. I'll see you soon."

The wall went dark. Andrew turned around. "Matt, my friend, we must see my family!"

"Sounds good to me. I guess I can always watch this episode in a few years when we get home."

Andrew and Matt went downstairs to the lobby. They found the LobbyTech and asked for transportation. Moments later, the LobbyTech called Andrew over to let him know his ride had arrived.

"Is there a cost for the ride?" Andrew asked.

"No, sir," the Tech said. "When I told them it was for Andrew Barton, they said it was complimentary."

Andrew thanked him, and he and Matt went to the

waiting vehicle. The door opened automatically for them, and they climbed in the back. Much to Andrew's surprise, there was no driver. He looked out the window to see if the driver had left the vehicle but didn't see anyone there.

"Welcome, Mr. Barton and Mr. Berman," a voice announced. The voice sounded as if it was coming from all around, but neither Andrew nor Matt could see any speakers.

"Uh, thank you?" Andrew said.

"Where can I take you today?" the voice replied.

Andrew read off the information on the paper in his hand. There was silence for a moment, and then the voice said, "Excellent sir. Please sit back and enjoy the ride. You are welcome to watch videos or listen to music. Food and drink are available at your request."

Matt asked, "Can I watch the episode of Dallas that I was watching before I left the hotel?"

"Of course, sir," the voice replied, and a screen appeared hovering in the air in front of Matt.

Andrew watched as Matt settled back and smiled at the action on the screen.

"Is there sound?" Andrew asked.

"What? Do you want me to turn it down?" Matt yelled.

Andrew shook his head, and Matt was reabsorbed into his television world.

Andrew said out loud, "I wonder why I can't hear it?"

The disembodied voice that seemed to be both host and driver answered, "It's tuned so that only the viewer can hear it. I can expand the audio so you can hear it if you'd like."

"No, thank you," Andrew said, looking up. "So, do I call you anything? Do you have a name?"

"Rob," the voice said.

"Okay, Rob," Andrew started. "Can I ask you questions? Do you make conversation?"

"Of course. If you'd like," Rob answered. "Do you have something in particular that you'd like to discuss, or would you like me to pick a subject?"

"I'd like to know about the Barton museum hours. When does it open and close?"

"It's open all the time. Most businesses are open twenty-four hours per day year-round. Because jobs and leisure times differ, businesses adapted years ago to ensure everyone can experience all businesses whenever convenient. The only exception is when auto mechanical maintenance is taking place. That is generally announced well in advance for a business, as each has yearly maintenance schedules. Then the business is closed for about an hour depending on the maintenance's complexity and the business's size."

"Thank you, Rob," Andrew said. "When is the next shutdown for the museum?"

"I'm sorry, sir," Rob said, "but we have arrived at your destination. Thank you for choosing to ride with Robinson Transxi. Your current fare is…zero dollars…"

With that, the doors opened, and Matt's screen vanished, eliciting loud moans, groans, and protests from Andrew's friend.

Andrew and Matt exited the vehicle and stepped away, watching as it sped down the road.

"Well, that was exciting," Matt said. "I'm never going to see the end of this episode, though."

"Maybe Jolena has a television inside," Andrew said, looking at the house. The outside of the house looked like a blank white wall. He saw no windows or doors, but a pathway led from the street to the building, so Andrew started walking toward the house. Matt followed.

"Weird-looking building," Matt said. "Where are the windows?"

As they reached the side of the home, a door slid open, and out bounced Jolena. She wrapped her arms around Andrew in a big hug and then held him at arm's length, studying him as if she were welcoming home a long-lost friend. "I've looked forward to this day for so long! It said in the book that it would happen, but I thought it was just a story!" Jolena said. "Please come in. Let me get you some hot cocoa."

Matt said, "Hot cocoa? Uh, isn't it a little warm for that right now?"

Jolena looked at Matt and smiled. "It's never too hot for cocoa, silly." She turned and walked toward the house.

Andrew turned to Matt and mimicked, "Silly." He smiled and ran toward the house with Matt in close pursuit.

Andrew and Matt sat in a comfortable front room area. The sofa's unique fabric conformed to various body parts, making it very comfortable.

Jolena returned with her cocoa and set the cups on the table. Coasters immediately appeared under the cups. Matt grabbed his cup and sipped carefully at the hot liquid. His eyes grew wide.

"This is the best hot cocoa I've ever had!" he said. "Andrew, you've got to try this."

Andrew picked up his cup and tasted the warm liquid inside of it. He closed his eyes and smiled. "Reminds me of home," he said. "It tastes just like what Julie makes."

Jolena smiled. "Old family recipe. Now I know where it came from!"

Andrew took another sip and set his cup on the table. "I'm going to let this cool just a little. In the meantime, Jolena, what can you tell us about this book I keep hearing about?"

"Well," Jolena said, thinking, "many books were written about you, but this particular book was the first. It was deemed to be the most accurate. The funny thing is, since you showed up, some of the writing has changed, and it just keeps changing. Your theory of changing timelines seems to play out while you're here."

"Was that theory mentioned at the beginning of the book?"

"Uh huh," Jolena said, sipping her cocoa.

"So, you said that Stephanie wrote the book?" Andrew asked, picking up his cup.

"Yeah," she said, "you used to sit at night and tell her the stories of your adventures, so she decided to write them down."

"And the book is still here? I mean. You still have the book?" Andrew asked.

"Yeah. It's in my bedroom. But I can't show it to you. The beginning of the book warns us not to ever show you the book because if you knew what was to come, it might change things too much. I hope you understand."

"I do understand," Andrew said. "It's actually a smart thing to think about. I was wondering about the book still being here because when I left, I hadn't started telling Stephanie about my adventures yet. You said that the words in the book were changing since I've been here, so what that means to me is that I will somehow get back to my time.”

“Oh yeah,” Jolena chuckled. “The last time I looked, you just got in the POD and returned, but now it’s all like secret agent stuff. It’s pretty cool. It might change even more because it said something about not knowing exactly what you wanted to do and not making up your mind until the last minute so they wouldn’t find out.”

“Yup,” he said and finished what was in his cup. “That’s the plan. So what do you do, Jolena? What kind of job do you have?”

“I’m a Magno-Solarian,” Jolena said matter-of-factly. “I really became interested in your work when I was young and was easily able to go into that field in college.”

“So you do something with the sun?” Matt asked.

“Magno-Solarians study the magnetic fields of the sun and monitor their flux. The sun has the strongest lines of force nearby, and they can easily affect how our machines work, everything from our cars to our spacecraft. It’s important to monitor the fields and calculate compensations for future flare-ups.”

“That’s interesting and makes sense,” Andrew said. “What are the predictions for today?”

“Nothing unusual,” Jolena said. “Pretty much just a normal day. Why do you ask?”

“I need to find a way to return to my POD and then return to my own time. Do you think that you could help me do that?”

Jolena became very quiet. “I don’t think I could do anything to help you. Besides, I’m sure the government monitors the book and watches how it changes. I really don’t want to lose my job or my freedom, but at the same time, I really want to be true to my family." She sat quietly, thinking about her choices.

"Just don't tell anyone about what you're going to do until you get home, or think about making up something," Matt said.

"That's it!" Andrew exclaimed. "Matt, my friend, sometimes you amaze me."

"Sometimes I amaze myself," Matt smiled.

"I don't understand," Jolena said.

"Let's go out," Andrew said cheerily. "Maybe you could show us around a little more. We already had the official tour, but I'd love to see what has happened to my old haunts, and I'm sure Matt would, too."

"Oh yeah. I wouldn't mind heading out to see what's still here and how much it's changed. Maybe we could even visit Sus…" Matt stopped in mid-sentence. "Never mind. I forgot where and when we were."

Andrew put his hand on Matt's shoulder. "We'll get back, buddy," he said. "I have a plan."

CHAPTER 16

The Book Lies

Matt, Andrew, and Jolena all went out and talked about the past and the present, present. Andrew learned many things about what had happened between then and now, although he and Matt, for whatever reason, kept most of that a secret until the day they died.

Jolena showed Andrew and Matt what had happened to several of the places where they used to hang out and then showed them places where most people their age went for fun these days.

At the Governor's Mansion, the Governor's secretary slowly opened the door to the Governor's office and stood quietly while the Governor finished her phone conversation.

"I don't care what they think; this is my state, and I'll run it how I see fit until I'm no longer in office. Is that clear?" She slammed her hand on her desk and disconnected the call from her desk viewer. After taking a deep breath, she became aware of her secretary standing in the room. "Yes? What is it?"

"I'm sorry to interrupt you, Madam Governor, but you asked me to inform you if there were any changes in The Book."

"I'm assuming from the fact that you're just standing there that there are indeed changes then?" the Governor asked, annoyed.

"Yes, ma'am. Sorry ma'am. The chapters involving our time have gone blank after Mr. Barton arrived."

"WHAT!" the Governor screamed, standing behind her desk, knocking over her chair. "Where is Barton now?"

"The last thing the book said was that he was visiting his relative, and they went sightseeing."

"We must find him. How the book was changed seemed to be the best history we could have hoped for. If he goes back and accidentally goes to that, that place as it was told, then our time will change. Call the Chief of Detectives and tell him I want to see him immediately!"

"Yes, ma'am," the secretary said, returning to her desk.

It didn't take long for Roger Benton, the Chief of Detectives, to arrive. Slightly out of breath, he ran into the Governor's office.

"I got here as fast as I could," he huffed.

"I expected you five minutes ago, but that's water under the bridge. I need you to find Andrew Barton and ensure he's not stealing back his POD. The book says that he's visiting his relative, Jolena. Take as many officers as you need and get over there. Find him. Detain him. Make sure that he does not go to the museum. Is that clear?"

"Yes, ma'am," Roger said.

Roger walked out of the room and grumbled to

himself.

He went straight back to the police station and immediately started to assemble a battalion of officers. He wanted to make sure that he picked the right people for the job, officers who had worked with celebrities in the past and weren't star-struck to the point where they couldn't do what was required of them. He gathered the officers together and briefed them regarding what they were about to do.

"Gentlemen, the assignment we have received is of utmost importance. To preface this, I need to tell you you are going to meet Andrew Barton." There was a collective gasp from the room and some murmuring that followed. When that had died down, he asked, "Is there anyone who feels they can't do this job and do it to the best of your abilities?"

No one raised their hands, and he wasn't sure if they didn't want to admit it or just pass up the chance to meet this remarkable man. He took them at their word and assigned them vehicles and positions.

Even though he was confident in the team he had chosen, he wondered if they could really live up to their responsibilities.

One officer approached him. "Sir?" he said.

Roger stopped and rubbed his eyes.

"Yes, Carl," he said. "What is it?"

"The team wanted me to ask you a question."

"I asked if there were any questions before dismissing all of you, and no one raised their hand," Roger said, slightly annoyed. He knew that the Governor would be monitoring his progress, and he didn't want any delays to affect what could possibly be an advancement in his career.

"No sir," the officer said and then looked down.

"Then what did they want you so desperately to ask about?" Roger was losing patience.

"Well, sir," he said. "It's just that the other officers were wondering if we don't have to arrest Mr. Barton, would it be appropriate to ask for his autograph or even have photos taken with him?"

Roger wasn't angry anymore. In fact, he had to try very hard not to laugh. In all honesty, he had wondered the very same thing. In fact, he had gone so far as to wonder if Mr. Barton would sign autographs for his children and wife. He shook his head slightly and looked at the nervous officer in front of him. "Tell them that if, and only if, we don't have to arrest Mr. Barton, they are welcome to ask for autographs, photos, and anything else he agrees to."

The officer smiled, relieved and happy at the answer. "Yes, sir! Thank you, sir!"

He ran off to tell the others, and Roger felt a wave of relief wash over him. His team was human, after all.

CHAPTER 17

The Plan

Andrew, Matt, and Jolena sat together in the closest thing they could find to a sports bar. Matt was still fascinated by the smart glasses that allowed him to have whatever drinks he wanted just by talking to them.

"Watch this," Matt said. "Rum and Coke." He poured the water into the glass, and a dark liquid filled it. He tasted it and said, "This is the best alcoholic beverage I've ever had!"

"You always say that, Matt," Andrew said. "Why don't you slow down a little? I'm going to need your help with this plan."

"But you're driving," Matt pouted. "I should be able to enjoy myself with what little time we have left here."

"I need you to be alert, and I certainly don't want to have to carry you into the POD when we get there."

"So, what is your plan? We haven't really talked about it," Jolena said.

"I can't tell you the plan, or it will appear in the book. You'll have to trust me on this. You said that you had a friend that could possibly help us?"

"Yeah. Malder Berken. He and I used to go out. I broke it off with him, but he's still enamored with me and would do anything to get me back. He's a MainTech and does maintenance on business maintenance systems." Jolena suddenly smiled. "Not only could he help you, but I'll bet he could show you a few things to help you out when you arrive home."

"That would be great!" Andrew said.

"But," Jolena became serious, "how will you keep the police from catching you? Your face is pretty well known, and I suspect they will be watching for you at the museum."

"This is the beauty of it. I will be having hot cocoa at your house the entire time I'm taking back my POD."

Jolena looked confused and felt even more so. "Okay, mister magic man. How will you do that?"

"It will mean that I must crack down on myself and start keeping notes. My plan is really pretty simple. After I meet your friend, I will send you home." Andrew paused and thought about what he was saying, "Sometime in the future," and then chuckled, "Well, my future is in the past; anyway, I'll come back here to visit you at this time. So, when the police try to find me, I'll be at your house. After they leave, I'll go back home. By coming back to visit during this exact time, I'll be able to be in two places at once."

The confused look on Jolena's face never really left. "So, you'll be in two places at once because you'll be visiting here twice at the same time?"

"Yeah. I'll just leave at different times during my lifetime. So how do we get in touch with this friend of yours?" Andrew felt a tapping on his shoulder. Still sitting next to him, Matt raised his hand in the air when Andrew turned.

"I have a question," Matt blurted out.

"What's that buddy?"

"Am I going to get hot cocoa, too?"

"We'll see," Andrew laughed. "If you end up coming back with me, then maybe we can all just have some when we get home and tell everyone about this adventure."

"Deal!" Matt said, finishing the rest of his drink.

Andrew chuckled and turned back to Jolena. "Now, how do we get in touch with this friend of yours?"

The sign outside the museum indicated that it would be undergoing routine maintenance and that sections throughout the building would close temporarily during the cycle. Andrew and Matt found it interesting that everything was always open, including holidays. Matt loved the fact that he would be able to go out any time of the day or night and date. Andrew thought about what shift he would have if he lived here and then realized that his job would be obsolete as intelligent machines did all of the routine things in life. Most people did technical jobs, although there were still doctors who interacted with people. Many stores had greeters and guides that would help you find what you needed should you choose to come see what they had. Most things were purchased via thought sets, small units placed in hats or visors that transmitted your thoughts to the appropriate store ordering systems. Even deliveries were done automatically. Andrew wondered how much of this came from his tinkering but was happy to know that his inventions changed transportation. He wondered about space travel and if he, through the use of his POD, would ever be able to travel in space. *That might be what I work on next*, he thought to himself.

He was roused from his thoughts as a security drone rounded the corner of the building. Security drones scanned faces and identified people who were loitering. Facial recognition has come a long way, and anyone scanned by the drone would be run through the database, and their location recorded. If you were wearing a mask, the drone also used various magnetic resonance strengths to record your bone structure, teeth, and vital signs. Andrew walked up to and past the drone. It didn't scan you if there were no crimes in progress or if you were moving at an average rate of speed. He turned the corner and waited until he thought the drone had moved on. He then looked around the corner to see if Malder had arrived yet. He had forgotten that Matt was standing with him for the moment and realized that he left Matt in front of the museum. When Andrew looked around the corner, he saw Matt standing in front of the drone and talking to it.

Andrew motioned to Matt, trying to get him to walk away. Matt replied by waving furiously at Andrew and smiling. Andrew hit himself in the forehead and threw his hands in the air in an attempt to question what Matt was doing. As he watched, he saw a young man approach Matt and ask him some questions. Then, the young man turned to the drone and said something. The drone scurried around Matt and went down the street. When the man turned back toward Matt, Matt pointed to where Andrew was crouching by the corner of the building, and the young man started over. Andrew's heart raced, and he wondered what he would do next.

The young man rounded the corner and almost ran over Andrew, startling him. Andrew stood up and brushed himself off. "Dang shoelaces. They always seem to come untied at the strangest times."

The young man looked confused and looked down at Andrew's feet. "Shoelaces?" he asked. "I haven't heard of shoelaces in years. Haven't seen any ever!"

Andrew looked at the young man's shoes. They seemed to be held together with some sort of strap—maybe magnetic latches? He didn't know and really didn't care to ask at this point. "Well, I need to get going," Andrew said casually and started to walk away.

The young man stopped him, saying, "But aren't you, Mr. Barton? I'm Malder, Jolena's friend."

Andrew stopped and turned back around. "Why didn't you say so at first? I thought you were some undercover cop or something."

Malder laughed. "Far from being connected in any way with the police, Mr. Barton. I'm only in my twenties and still have a little bit of a rebellious streak. Why do you think I'm here helping you? It was the government who confiscated your POD, and now the government needs to see what individual citizens can do if they put their minds to it."

Some things just never change, Andrew thought and chuckled to himself. "Okay," he said, "I assume that we're not just going to march in there and let them know that I want to go home. So what's the plan?"

"Well, first, I think you need to get your friend over here so he can hear the plan as well," Malder said nodding toward Matt.

Andrew looked over at Matt, who was playing with a

pedestrian crossing button, and giggled.

"Is he okay?" Malder asked.

"He's just being Matt," Andrew laughed. "He's wonderfully naive but would do anything for a friend."

The plan was simple. Malder would go in through the front and tell the museum curator that he was doing a surprise inspection of the maintenance units and staying ahead of their care, especially since the museum now held a national and irreplaceable treasure. Matt and Andrew would wait by a rear access passage until Malder had the rooms sealed for the procedure. He would sneak them in, and they would leave.

"Ok," Malder said as they approached the side of the building. "This is where I want you to wait. I'll get you as soon as I have the rooms sealed."

Andrew nodded as Malder walked off.

Matt was never good at waiting for anything and became bored quickly. He wandered around the small area, exploring everything that he could find. "There's nothing to do," Matt complained. "How long is this going to take. I'm getting hungry."

"I'm hoping it won't be much longer," Andrew said. "I have to wonder, though, if I'm at Jolena's house right now and what I'm doing if I am there. I'll remember this later but won't know what's happening there."

Matt became very quiet, and Andrew turned to look at him. Matt was just staring at Andrew, his mouth open.

"I really think you've lost it, buddy," Matt said, shaking his head. "What the heck are you talking about?"

"Matt," Andrew said, "I know you were sitting right next to me when I told Jolena all about this, but I imagine you weren't listening. At least I'm pretty sure you weren't listening to everything I said."

"Yeah, I'm sure that was also the case because I'm lost now. Care to explain it to me?"

Andrew started to explain the concept of coming back during this time and how he hoped that he would be able to control his time travel better at some time in the future. While he was explaining this to Matt, he still wondered if it had worked out and what, if anything, his future self was doing right now.

The droid had run a facial recognition of Matt through the state database. It initially came back with no data, but when it was run through the confidential files, Matt's name showed up with alarming speed.

The police drove by the museum and contacted the curator to be on the lookout for any strangers lurking about. Not finding Matt or Andrew in the area, they moved on to the next logical location: Jolena's house. When the police arrived in full force, the lead detective led the way to the door. He announced loudly, overriding the privacy shield that hid the door from plain view of visitors and identified himself as a police officer, commanding her to open up. Just as they were about to break down the door, a very surprised Jolena opened it.

"May I help you?" she asked the detective.

"You can show us the whereabouts of Andrew Barton, immediately!"

"Um, why do you need to see Andrew?" she asked.

A nod from the detective was all it took for a battalion of officers to push through the door and fan out inside the house, ignoring Jolena's protests and legal threats. As he stepped up, the detective smiled and handed her a piece of official-looking paper.

"Search Warrant," he said smugly and waltzed into the foyer.

Jolena closed the door and looked at the paper as she walked toward the living room. "What exactly are you looking for?" she asked the detective.

"Andrew Barton. Is he here?" the detective asked.

"Well, um, Andrew is, um..."

"What's going on out there, Jolena?" A voice interrupted her.

She smiled and looked at the detective. "He's right in here," she said. Jolena turned the corner and saw Andrew sitting on the couch.

"I thought you were getting some hot cocoa," he said smiling, "but I see we have company."

Andrew stood, walked over to the detective, and stuck out his hand. "I'm Andrew Barton, and you are?"

The detective was stunned. After a brief hesitation, the detective grasped Andrew's hand, shook it, and said quietly, "Detective Roger Benton. Excuse me for a moment while I confirm your identity."

Roger took out a small, flat screen and pushed an almost invisible button on his sleeve. A picture of Andrew popped up. Roger looked at the photo and held it beside Andrew's face. "You look a little older than the picture," Roger said.

Andrew looked at the photo. "When was this taken?" he asked.

"I'm not sure. It's the only one we have on file."

"Well then," Andrew laughed. "It must be the photo

from my book. I must have been in my twenties then, but," Andrew stretched the skin on his face, "we all age somewhat as we get older. Besides, I'm a time traveler, and that tends to do strange things to a person. Do you time travel at all, Roger?"

Roger shook his head. "I have never met a time traveler before, so I wouldn't know what it does to a person other than move them through time."

Andrew laughed again, "I'll have to remember that one," he said, turning toward Jolena. "Do you have enough cocoa to make a cup for everyone? I have many stories that I would love to tell these fine folks."

"I'll get started," Jolena smiled and walked to the kitchen.

As they all entered the living room to sit down, Roger asked, "Excuse me for asking this, but I have to. My job, you know. Where is your traveling companion, Matt?"

Andrew leaned close to Roger and whispered, "You'll have to forgive Matt. He wasn't feeling well. I think he has the flu. He's been in the bathroom for quite a while."

Roger motioned to an officer and whispered, "Would you please go and check the bathroom to ensure Matt is okay?"

The officer nodded and walked down the hall. He came to a closed door and tried the knob. It was locked, but a voice from inside responded to the handle, turning, "Hey buddy, can you please use the other bathroom? I'm still not doing well." The request was immediately followed by the unpleasant sound of major regurgitation.

The officer turned up his nose and walked quickly back to the living room. He walked over to Roger and said,

"He's in there and really sounds sick. I suggest we give him all the time he needs."

Roger nodded, then pressed another button on the small panel incorporated into his suit sleeve. Andrew watched with fascination at the motions. "Is that like some kind of keyboard or something?"

"This?" Roger asked, pointing to the series of buttons on his sleeve. "Yes. It actually connects directly to the police department computer. I just sent your photo to the database along with one I took of you while comparing you to the photo."

"Amazing!" Andrew said. "You'll have to tell me more about that after my stories are done. Do you all have some time when we can visit? I'm sure I can tell you a few stories about me that aren't in your book."

All of the officers looked pleadingly at Roger, who smiled and shook his head slightly. He had to admit that he was excited to hear some stories no one knew. Stories that he could share and give himself a little notoriety. Roger nodded and said, "Okay. We can stay for a few stories, but then we all need to get back to work." The others cheered, hearing this, and settled into their seats as Jolena brought out trays of hot cocoa. Andrew smiled to himself. He knew how this would play out already as he started his story. "Let me tell you about the time I came into a future world that no one knows about. A world much like this one..."

CHAPTER 18

Check

Back at the museum, Matt had just realized what Andrew was saying and smiled broadly. "I get it now. You're here and there!"

"But not everywhere," Andrew replied.

Matt laughed. "That's a good one. Here and there, but not everywhere. Good thing you're not. I wouldn't know who was the real you and who wasn't. The real you, I mean."

Andrew smiled. "I understand Matt." He looked around and said out loud, "I wonder if Malder is having problems. Seems like he's been in there a long time."

"You know what bothers me?" Matt didn't wait for an answer. "It bothers me that there is no door here. Where are we supposed to be going in?"

As if to answer his question, the building's wall suddenly shook slightly and formed a doorway. Once the doorway was formed, the slab of wall that made up the doorway slid slowly into the ground, leaving an opening into the museum. A smiling Malder appeared.

"You guys can come in now," Malder said. After a moment of hesitation, which allowed their initial shock to wear off, Matt and Andrew carefully walked through the doorway. Andrew had the urge to step over the opening. His mind told him that a wall had just sunk into the ground, and he didn't want to have his foot on that spot should the wall decide to come back up at that moment. Once they were both inside the room, Malder waved his hand over a piece of the wall directly next to the opening, and the doorway sealed itself up again.

Matt whistled. He walked over to where the doorway had been and squared his shoulders. "Open says me!" he commanded. When nothing happened, he waved furiously at the spot where Malder had just waved to close the doorway. Malder stifled a laugh. Matt turned and looked at Malder and asked, "How did you do that?"

Malder showed him the ring on his right hand. "This is a secured transmitter. When you wave it over the close-range receiver at the proper speed, it starts the opening or closing sequence. It can only be done from the inside."

Matt looked closely at the ring. "Sure beats my garage door opener at home."

"Yes," Malder said, gently taking his hand back. He turned to Andrew. "I believe that the curator was somewhat suspicious, but I convinced him that this was official due to the nature of the materials being held here, namely, your POD. He was most insistent on staying in the room during the process. Still, after I told him of other owners who also insisted and were no longer with us due to the unpredictable nature of the machines and their actions, he quickly remembered some other things that needed his attention."

"I'm glad!" Andrew sighed in relief.

"But, we will have to act quickly. I'm not entirely convinced that the police aren't out looking for you right now," Malder said.

"I'm hoping that they are and that they found me," Andrew replied to a very confused Malder.

Matt smiled and said, "I can explain it to him." He opened his mouth, looked at Andrew, and said, "Never mind. If you explain it to him, I'll listen this time."

Andrew sighed.

Malder said, "Explain it to me as we go. I've only closed a small part of the museum, and we must keep up with the maintenance machines. If things are not done correctly, the entire system shuts down, and all the doors open. The main computer assumes that the MainTech has been injured and needs help. When we get to your POD, we'll only have about twenty minutes to get you and Matt inside and back home before the program finishes."

"It won't even take me that long to get out of here if they haven't messed with the computer or the coordinates at all," Andrew said.

Malder looked amused and said, "I'm not sure there is anyone, anywhere in this time, that would even begin to understand your computer. It's pretty big and bulky. We have kids' computers that could outthink what you have. I'll have to tell you a few things to remember when you go back. It might help a little. Maybe I'll be part of why some of your inventions are invented." Malder smiled at the thought, and Andrew felt there might be more truth to that statement than he knew.

Andrew had hoped that getting from point 'A,' where they had entered the building, to point 'B,' where his POD was located, would allow him to see more of the museum. The reality was that he would see only the room in which his POD was being stored. Malder carefully led them through a series of well-hidden passages in the walls. These were service tunnels that only the techs used when running maintenance sequences and revealed none of the museum's interior.

As they carefully made their way through the tunnels, Andrew questioned Malder about several things he had seen during his stay. He wondered how things worked and on what theory they were based. He was especially interested in the panels and instruments that allowed Malder to control things in the tunnels with such a small device as his ring. Malder went on and on about everything that Andrew asked about. Matt made faces and hated being in the smallish tunnels. Although he wasn't claustrophobic, he was uncomfortable enough to get the feeling he was running out of air. Matt would frequently stop, much to the dismay of Malder. Matt would assure everyone that he was doing fine and that they should go on without him. He would clutch his chest, hang his head, and motion them away with his hand in dramatic gestures. Andrew just smiled and assured Matt that they would never leave him behind. He wasn't sure what Malder thought, except that he was becoming impatient.

They made their way through the seemingly endless maze of tunnels when, to Matt's relief, Malder drew a line on a wall, which opened, much like the one that let them into the building.

The three of them stepped out into a large room. Malder had cautioned them to stay close to the opening, and when they looked around, they saw various machines moving rapidly from spot to spot, with other machines following them. Andrew wondered if they had an endless supply of machines to care for and if any people ever did the manual labor to fix or maintain the machines.

Andrew looked around the room and noticed a section across from where they were standing that looked very much like the inside of his garage. There were a few items out of place and several different variations of what, he was sure, they thought was correct for the time period. However, Andrew noticed that many of the items were slightly more modern than he would have had in his time. He wondered if all historians fudged like this in displays. Guess it didn't really matter. After all, who would know other than a time traveler?

In the replica of his garage sat the one thing he felt was authentic and the prize he was searching for; his POD and his ticket home. He started to ask Malder how long it would take, but Malder raised a finger to his mouth. Within a few seconds, the machines scampered to the corners of the rooms and vanished into the walls. Malder then walked out into the center of the room and smiled. "Your ship awaits you, sir!" he said with a mock bow and a grin.

Andrew walked out to stand next to Malder. He couldn't believe that he was going home. There was a sense of sadness, yet he somehow knew he'd be back someday, so the sadness was only fleeting. He turned to Malder. "Thank you for helping me to get home. I miss my family. When I arrive back home, it should be only a second or so from when I left. It always seems strange to me that I can be gone for hours or even days and live this life where I really miss home, and yet no one misses me there because, to them, it's like I never left."

Malder put his hand on Andrew's shoulder. "I can't imagine ever getting used to that. What would happen, then, if you could never go home?"

Andrew thought. "I guess time would move on without me at some point. It probably does anyway, but when I return, no one remembers because my arrival is before anyone can worry or even know I've left. The whole thing is very strange to think about, so I try not to. I just know when I leave and when I should return."

While Andrew and Malder were being philosophers of different times, Matt had walked over to the POD, eager to get home. Andrew looked over at his friend, who had just opened the POD door. Matt gazed into the POD's interior, his mouth wide and his body motionless. He slowly turned toward Andrew and said, "I think we might have a problem, buddy."

Andrew and Malder walked quickly to the POD and looked inside. Andrew's stomach sank. The woman sitting inside the POD smiled and glared at the same time. Malder smirked. "Madam Governor," he said, "what a disappointment to see you here."

The Governor sat quietly as if thinking, then said to Andrew, "Mr. Barton, it might surprise you to know that I'm not here to stop you. I'm actually here to encourage you to leave. You see, I want to go with you. I want you to take me back to your time."

CHAPTER 19

Check Mate

In Jolena's living room Andrew continued his story while several police officers and the detective listened intently.

"As I was saying, I came to a future world much like this one, but no one knew of it. They didn't know about it because in the realm of reality, it really didn't exist except for a very short time. The reason the world existed at all was partly my fault. If I had never shown up, this world would have been much different. I realized this through other travels into the future beyond so I set out to correct, as best I could, the error I had made. Why, all of humanity depended on it! It was a very heavy burden to bear. Finally, one day, I was able to make it back to the exact time I had hoped, and being there, I was able to cause a distraction just long enough to allow myself on a previous visit to escape back in time, thus setting the time line back on the right course. Of course, it really wasn't entirely that simple. I had to go back and correct other things in other times, but eventually, things were set straight."

Roger was suspicious and narrowed his eyes at

Andrew. "When," Roger swallowed hard, "exactly was this time?" As he asked the question, his clothing changed from the suit he was wearing, to a more casual look with no jacket and blue jeans. Andrew smiled to himself.

Several officers vanished and others reappeared in their places. Jolena watched in amazement as she sat next to Andrew seeing the changes unfold around her. Even though she found herself being aware of what was going on, she felt as if everything was the way it should be.

Andrew said, "It was the here and now, Roger."

Roger stood and ordered the officers to go check the bathroom. As two officers rushed down the hallway, two more stood on either side of Andrew. "Please get up," Roger said to him.

Andrew stood and was escorted down the hallway to the closed bathroom door.

The lead officer pounded on the door and shouted, "Mr. Berman! You need to open the door!"

Andrew said quietly, "You can open the door, officer. It's not locked and no one is in there."

The amazed officer turned the knob and carefully went inside, searching the small room for occupation. He came out and looked at Roger. "There's no one there, sir."

Roger looked at Andrew. His face was red with anger, but he spoke as calmly as he could. "Where is Mr. Berman?"

"Matt, um, was never here. At least the Matt that would have been with me on this trip was not here. The voice you heard earlier came from a small device I have with me that displaces sound waves to coordinates of my choosing. So I played back Matt's voice and chose to have it come from inside the bathroom."

Roger was beyond words. Andrew stood calmly, trying not to laugh at the situation.

"If I have my way about it, Mr. Barton, you will never see the light of day again as long as you live. You may never even see the inside of a courtroom. I might just take you to the prison and drop you off and tell the Warden never to let you out. EVER! One more thing, Mr. Barton..."

Andrew anticipated that fluctuations in the time line were still stabilizing, and watched as each change took place. This one even took Andrew by surprise though. Roger stopped, briefly for a moment in mid-sentence. As he watched, Andrew saw Rogers outfit change again to a business casual look. Several of the police officers vanished and the ones that remained, had a change of clothing as well. The police uniforms changed into dark suits. Earpieces adorned their ears, and dark sunglasses appeared on their faces. When Roger continued speaking it was exactly what Andrew hoped to hear.

"One more thing, Mr. Barton," Roger repeated in a jovial tone, "you had better plan on visiting us again!" Roger put his hand on Andrew's shoulder. "Our historians are enamored with you and love spending time to make sure that our histories are correct."

"I'm planning on coming back in six months from now to visit again," Andrew said smiling.

"Are you sure you won't share the secret of time travel with us? It could be an amazing help to our society."

Andrew laughed. "Maybe someday when I know that I have all the bugs worked out. For now it's, well, still a little iffy. Let's see how things go with my next visit."

A man in one of the dark suits leaned over to Roger

and whispered, "Governor, we have a tight schedule today. We should be leaving soon."

"Yes, of course," Roger said. "That's my cue to leave, but I'm looking forward to our next get together."

"Thank you, Governor," Andrew said. "It's also my cue to leave now. Thank you so much for your hospitality!"

Andrew smiled and twisted the ring on his finger just before he waved it over his belt buckle. As he did so, he faded and vanished.

Roger shook his head and said aloud to no one in particular, "I sure wish that I could do that!" He thanked a very confused Jolena for her hospitality and left the house.

When they were gone and Jolena shut the door, she looked in the air and said, "You have a lot of explaining to do Andrew Barton, the next time you come back."

CHAPTER 20

Rematch

Andrew stared into the POD.

"Governor," he said, "I honestly don't know what would happen to the timeline if I took you back with me. I don't even know what would happen to you if I took you back to a time before you were born. I don't have theories about that."

"I don't care!" the Governor stood up and walked to the entrance of the POD. Andrew watched as her business attire shifted slightly and changed to more casual wear.

"Whoa!" Matt said. "What was that?"

"I don't know," Andrew said, confused.

"I don't care what might happen." the Governor said. "I've never felt right here. I've always felt out of place and in the wrong era. I want to go back to a simpler time. If you want to take the POD, you'll have to take me with you."

Andrew started to pace and spoke out loud, trying to figure out what to do. "I can't be responsible for your safety,

Governor. I'm not even sure what it would do to us! I can't risk hurting either myself or Matt. This is a bad situation."

"You have no choice, Mr. Barton," the Governor said. "If you don't agree to take me, I will have a platoon of secret service here before you can blink. Then neither of us will get to your time."

Andrew stopped pacing and stood quietly, then resigned, "I guess I have no choice but to honor your request."

"You do have a choice, Andrew. Taking her back would be a grave mistake." The voice seemed familiar to Andrew and yet strange at the same time. Before he could look toward this new voice, he heard Matt say, "Either I'm going crazy, or the evil Andrew is back!" (The 'evil Andrew' was a version of Andrew from a different timeline, a cautionary tale of what he could become if he made certain choices.)

He was a little taken aback when Andrew finally saw who had spoken. "Who are you?" he asked.

"I'm you, Andrew. Only, I'm you from ten years in your future."

Andrew felt a little lightheaded at first but then realized that this was what he had hoped would happen, only he didn't expect to see it.

The older Andrew spoke. "It's extraordinary. I remember all of this happening. I remember how it will end and what I was thinking then. Weird looking back on this and reliving it from this perspective. No, Matt. You're not going crazy, and I'm not the evil Andrew. Actually, though, you'll be dealing with him soon enough." He chuckled a little. "Andrew, remember that not all inventions that enter your mind must become a reality." He turned back to Matt and said, "In the time I come from, Matt, you've made some great strides in life. You'll be far from crazy, but I don't want to influence how you'll get to where you'll be, so let's focus on the present, at least where we are now."

"I know," Matt said calmly. "I end up with Susie, raising a family and becoming the head of a major corporation that funds all your projects."

Everyone stared. The older Andrew looked somewhat uncomfortable, and the younger Andrew wondered how close Matt had come to being right.

The Governor cleared her throat, and all eyes turned toward her. While in conversation with the older Andrew, the Governor's clothing had changed again. Her hair was down, and she looked much younger and less stressed. The younger Andrew even found her to be attractive.

"So, am I going to be able to go back with you?" she asked.

The younger Andrew replied, "Governor, as I said before, I don't know the ramifications of taking you back with me."

"First of all, Mr. Barton," she said, "I'm not the Governor, and I don't know why you keep calling me that. You can either call me Miss Sorenson or Lydia. Second, I don't see how taking me back to your time will affect me as long as you bring me back to a time close to where we are now."

"Now I know I'm going crazy," Matt mumbled. He walked over to Malder, who had been standing quietly the entire time and not knowing what to say. Matt put his arm around the confused young man and said, "Don't worry. It's not always like this. Just most of the time. You never quite get used to it. You can only accept it."

The older Andrew said, "Lydia, taking you back in the POD would have devastating effects. In most timelines, going back means you never have a family and that is the key to all of this. There is another timeline, however, I believe you'll find palatable. I have developed the technology to take you with me to a few pre-planned destinations that I'm sure you would love to visit. You are an archaeologist, yes?"

"I am, indeed," she sparkled in her response. "My fiancé is also an archaeologist."

"Yes, I know," the older Andrew commented. "I believe his name is Richard Anselm. At the risk of revealing a few things, your grandson will go on to make intergalactic history, so you must return here and nurture that relationship with Richard. In the meantime, you can go with me, and we'll let my younger self get back to where he needs to be."

"I can live with that," Lydia said. "I'm sorry I tried to stow away on your POD, Andrew. I'm glad that we've met and have had time to talk. I hope you'll come back again so we can talk more. It's fascinating hearing about the past from someone who is currently from there."

"Thank you. Apparently, I'll be back more often than I imagine. I hope to see you again." At that statement, Andrew realized that he would. He turned to his older self and walked over to speak quietly.

"I'm glad that this worked out. Is there any advice you can give me to help me get to where you are now?" The younger Andrew wondered how much he could be told without damaging his timeline.

"Young man," his older self said, "there's not much I

can tell you at all, and I know you're wondering about that. I am going to tell you that your next adventure is going to be a difficult one. You'll need all the help you can get, and if you think things through, you'll make it to where I am today. If not, then I'm unsure how this will all play out. Just remember that self-sacrifice does not always have to end up badly. Sometimes, the ultimate sacrifice ends up with new life and new creations. It's not always the end of things. Remember that when the time comes. If you can do what I remember happening the way it happened, everything will be all right. Good luck." Older Andrew started to turn but then looked back at the younger Andrew. "I know you're curious about why Lydia's clothes continued to morph. It has to do with the places I take her and her continuing evolution in this time. With each place she visits she changes a little more."

The older Andrew turned to Lydia and said, "Shall we go? Michelangelo awaits."

Lydia beamed with delight, like a small child about to embark on her first visit to the carnival. Andrew indicated that she should stand next to him. "Good luck," he said to his younger self. He adjusted his ring, and passed it over his belt buckle. Within a moment, both he and Lydia had vanished.

The room was silent, and no one moved, not believing the sight before them.

Malder was the first to speak up. "I'm not sure what just happened, but I'm pretty sure that we need to get you into the POD before someone comes in. The maintenance cycle is over, and the doors are opening."

Andrew looked around to see the doors unlatching and opening. Behind the doors, numerous people were crowding to get in. His heart sank, and he grabbed Matt. "We need to get going, buddy." As they started toward the opening of the POD, a voice cut through the crowd's murmuring. "There he is!"

Andrew knew his chance to escape was gone as the crowd pushed into the room. A tall, official-looking man approached the front and stood before Andrew. Andrew waited for what he knew would be a reprimand and steeled himself for the worse.

To his surprise, the tall man wrapped his arms around Andrew and hugged him. "Thank you for coming to visit," the man said. "We will miss you."

The crowd broke out into applause and cheering. Matt, always adaptable to situations, smiled and waved, basking in the moment's glory.

The tall man turned toward the crowd and held up his hands to silence the outburst of noise. When all was quiet, he cleared his throat. "As Mayor of this community, I want to thank all of you for coming out to see this historic occasion. To my knowledge, none of us here have ever traveled in time. None but these two brave young souls, who come to us from a time long past to share their knowledge, nay, their wisdom with us here in their future. We learn from the past and from our mistakes and successes. We are privileged to have been able to interact with Mr. Barton and look forward to his return." The tall man, who was the Mayor, turned to Andrew. Another man, presumably the Mayor's aide, handed the Mayor a large key. The Mayor handed it to Andrew. "Please accept this key to our fair city. You will always be welcome anyplace you go here whenever you choose to return." The Mayor looked up amidst gentle flashes and whirring sounds and placed his arm around Andrew, motioning for Matt to join them. Although Andrew couldn't see the cameras, he knew they were somewhere. The Mayor continued in his booming, political voice. "And now, Mr. Barton, we eagerly await witnessing your return to your own time. Safe journey."

The Mayor motioned for people to move back. Others in the back stood on tiptoes to see more clearly. Andrew turned to the POD and stepped inside. Matt followed and, once inside, leaned out again, waving to a cheering crowd. "Goodnight, Colorado!" he yelled in his best rock and roll voice and was pulled inside by Andrew.

Andrew closed the door, and the POD powered up when he hit a few switches and started running a few sequences in the program.

"So, buddy," Matt said, beaming. "How do we get back?"

"Getting back is easy," Andrew said. "Do you want to do the honors?"

"Heck yeah!" Matt said. "What do I do?"

Andrew waited for the computer screen to light up. "Here's the password," he told Matt. "Once the desktop is up, simply press this icon on the screen. It begins the auto-return sequence. Five seconds after you press it, we should be back home to our original spot at the original time we left."

"So there's nothing I can do to screw this up?" Matt asked.

"Not if you just press this icon," Andrew said nervously.

Matt leaned over and said, "Here we go!"

He pressed the icon and quickly sat down. He briefly heard the crowd's cheering, which quickly faded to silence. "I'm gonna miss that," Matt said. "My five minutes of glory comes hundreds of years after I've died, but at least I was around to see it."

Andrew smiled and thought it odd that Matt said the same thing he had said earlier in the day. "You'll have many more times like today, my friend. I don't know about you, but I'm ready to see my family and get some rest. Maybe next weekend we can try something new and different. I'll modify the POD this week and hope we can all go on a short trip. It will be fun."

"You're right," Matt said, standing up. "I want to see Susie and tell her about my adventure."

"Think she'll believe you?" Andrew asked.

"I'm pretty sure she will," Matt said, "after I show her this." Matt reached into his pocket and took out a drinking glass.

"Matt!" Andrew exclaimed. "Is that a glass from the restaurant?"

"It sure is, buddy!" Matt smiled. "Now I can have whatever drink I want, whenever I want it, using just water."

"Huh," Andrew said and looked at the key to the city in his lap. "I'll be curious to see if it works since we brought it back before it was invented."

"Maybe it's because I brought it back that it gets invented. Did you ever think about that?"

"Could be. Don't break it," Andrew joked. "Hope it's dishwasher safe."

Andrew opened the door to the POD just as Julie stepped out into the garage from the kitchen.

"Hi, sweetheart," she said. "You and Matt working on the POD?" she asked.

"Just got back from a trip. I'd love to tell you all about

it."

"And I'd love to hear all about it as long as it wasn't another dimensional trip," she said, taking his hand and leading him into the house. Matt followed them in and announced that he was heading out. "Thanks for the peek into the future," he said as he shut the front door.

"The future?" Julie asked. "Tell me all about it, and next time, maybe I can go with you."

Andrew nodded and started to tell her everything about his adventure.

In the quiet of the garage, the voices whispered.

"I know now how to get his secret," one voice said.

"Then do it and bring him to me. I want that knowledge. With it, I can regain my rightful place as ruler and heir to the throne of earth."

CHAPTER 21

The Truth About You

As we go through life, we ask people for advice, seek out the knowledge of others, and look to those wiser than ourselves for guidance. When it all comes down to it, we must rely on ourselves and our experiences to make the final decisions. Sometimes, if we're sincere, we might not like the answers we provide ourselves. That's when the internal struggles commence. Often, we don't know what the right thing to do is, and that's when the strongest side of us, with the strongest influences, wins out.~ Andrew Barton

Andrew heard Julie's voice. It sounded distant and so much farther away than if she had been in the room with him. It sounded upset, and he didn't know why.

"What is wrong with you? I'm really getting worried about you. You're not like yourself at all today."

Andrew opened his eyes and squinted at the light streaming through the blinds in his bedroom window. He wondered who she was talking to. That's when he heard the voice.

"There's nothing wrong with me. I've just finally come to my senses. I know that I can no longer keep working on these ridiculous experiments. It's time that I saved our money to care for you and Stephanie."

Andrew sat up in bed. It was his voice that he heard. He jumped out of bed, pulled on some pants, threw on a T-shirt, and ran down the stairs.

He honestly didn't expect to see what he found in the living room, and it had to make him check his sanity when he arrived. There, in the living room, standing with Julie, was himself.

Julie heard the noise on the stairs and looked up. "What the…?" she said, looking back and forth between the two Andrews standing within her sight.

"Well," Andrew said on the steps, "it looks like I'm back." He carefully came down the stairs and stood next to Julie.

Julie couldn't stop looking at the two identical men. "I don't even know who to talk to anymore," she said.

Andrew, who had just descended the stairs, asked Julie, "Why don't you catch me up on what's happening here. Don't worry. I'm the Andrew you slept with all night, so let's call this young man Andrew 2."

"Maybe you should call me the sensible one," Andrew 2

grumbled.

Julie looked at Andrew and said, "I thought you had come downstairs while I was making breakfast. This Andrew started telling me that he's decided to stop experimenting and get rid of everything in the garage so that he can spend more time with Stephanie and me. He seems very intent on this happening. As good as that sounds, I don't want to see you set back in your work. You've accomplished so much and are close to exciting things. Andrew, who is this man?"

Andrew 2 looked at Julie with the same look that her husband gets when hurt. "You don't know me? You really don't know your own husband? Julie, that hurts me to the core of my being."

Andrew walked over to Andrew 2. "I think that you and I need to go out to the garage and chat," he said, taking Andrew 2 by the arm.

Andrew 2 shrugged. "Maybe I can talk some sense into you before it's too late," he said.

Julie watched as the two men walked out the kitchen door into the garage.

Andrew walked over and sat on his chair at the workbench. "Who are you?" he started. "Are you the person that was here earlier and wanted to destroy my POD?"

"I am that person," Andrew 2 said. "As for who I am, that's a bit more difficult of a question with no simple answer. You see, Andrew, I'm you. I'm your sensible side. At least, I feel like I'm your sensible side."

Andrew wasn't sure what to think. He felt fine. He felt as if he had sense, at least sense enough to ask the next question. "If you're me, where did you come from, and how did you get here?"

Andrew 2 began pacing. Andrew thought it strange to see himself pacing from another's point of view. Andrew 2 said, "As far as I can tell, you went on an experimental trip a few weeks ago to see if you could control which direction the POD goes in time. Do you remember that?"

"Yes, I do," Andrew said, "so how does that figure into all of this?"

Andrew 2 stopped pacing and looked at Andrew. "Try to have patience. I have to explain this as I see it and in ways that you might be able to understand." Andrew 2 continued pacing, and Andrew decided that he would no longer pace when he thought, as of today.

"As always, you went someplace you didn't expect to go. You ended up on a beach, which you assumed was on the coastline of this continent. You based this on the fact that there was oxygen, the sky was blue, and the ocean looked like, well, an ocean. What you didn't realize was that you had, once again, slipped sideways into another dimension. It was our earth, but not our earth. When you hit the return program, do you remember seeing a blur? Almost as if you had double vision?"

"Yes," Andrew said. "I wondered what it was but dismissed it as a side effect of traveling back."

"As it turns out, you hit an inter-dimensional ripple. A time speed bump, as it were. When you're in travel mode, your molecules are in flux. They aren't quite in any time but have become part of the fluid time stream. When you hit that bump, it jarred your molecules and separated them into another you. You must have hurried out of the POD and into the house when you returned home. I was set to return to the same location. Still, because the same molecules occupied the space where I was supposed to land, I somehow ended up in a future timeline when you were gone. I moved the POD so that there would be no chance of you not being able to return. I had come to realize that these experiments were dangerous and ridiculous. I tried to destroy your POD earlier since I now had the technology to travel without the POD. If I could save your life and your marriage, things would stop becoming so messed up with your timeline, and mine. I thought that by destroying the POD, you and I would rejoin."

"How could destroying the POD do that?" Andrew asked. "It doesn't make any sense."

"My theory is that the POD emits electromagnetic waves constantly disrupting the timeline. Destruction of the POD would stop that."

Andrew wasn't sure what to think. He wondered where this Andrew had stayed for the past few weeks and how he could move through time without the POD. He reasoned that this Andrew must have either been from the future or another dimension, but how did he know so much?

Andrew 2 continued, "Andrew, think of me as your voice of reason. I have seen that you will do some amazing things but also risk the lives of your friends and Julie to get what you want from these experiments. I want you to live a normal life. You need to get on caring for your family and being there for them. You need to stop spending the budget on ridiculous things."

Some things that Andrew 2 said really seemed to strike home, and yet there was something wrong with what he was saying. Andrew couldn't quite put his finger on it. As he thought about this, the door to the kitchen opened, and Matt, Susie, Kota, and Julie stepped out. Julie walked over to Andrew, who was sitting on the workbench chair.

"My Andrew, right?" She said to him.

Andrew 2 said, "We're both your Andrew, Julie, but one of us cares more about you and Stephanie."

Andrew said, "That's not true, and if you're really me, then you'll know that."

"And if I knew that, Andrew, then I wouldn't be here trying to end all of this foolishness!"

"I want a twin," Kota said.

Both Andrews turned to her and said simultaneously, "What?"

Kota giggled. "Yeah, just like that. They say twins think a lot alike and do the same things. I want someone who can be there and pretend to be me when I want to go out and do something fun."

Andrew 2 looked at Kota and said, "Thank you, Kota. You've just given me a great idea of making this work!" He turned to Andrew and said, "Ready for a game of hide and seek mixed with a game of tag?"

"What are you talking about?" Andrew asked, standing up.

"You'll see," Andrew 2 grinned. "Tag. You're it." Andrew 2 pressed the button on his belt and vanished.

Until then, everyone else in the garage had been quietly observing the bazaar scene of two Andrews.

"Did I say something bad, Mr. B?" Kota asked.

"No, no. Not at all. We're just dealing with an unstable version of myself, and we need to figure out how to stop him."

"What do you think he meant with the hide-and-seek and tag thing?" Susie asked.

"I'm not too sure," Andrew said thoughtfully. "I'm wondering what I would have meant if I said it to him."

"Well," Matt mused, "they are games. Maybe he's planning on playing a game with you, but he didn't tag you before he left, so that can't be it."

"No, no, Matt," Andrew said, snapping his fingers," I think you might be exactly right!"

"That he didn't tag you before he left?"

Andrew laughed, "That's a big part of it, I'm sure. You said something about it being a game. I think that's what it might be. A game!"

"What kind of game?" Susie asked.

"That's the better question," Andrew said. "I think I need to start working on a device to catch him, but not what he's wearing. Not the button on the belt thing."

"What are you going to try and make?" Julie asked.

"When Matt and I were in the future, my future self told me many things, and I noticed that he had something that connected his ring and belt. Two different devices that worked together. I'll start working on that."

"What are you going to do with it?" Susie asked.

"I'm going to play tag with him," Andrew replied. "I noticed once that when I was knocked back in time, I saw a ghost image of myself. This makes me believe that residual energy is left during a time or dimensional shift. I might use that to track my other self and follow where he goes. The only bad thing is that it might take me a few days to make something like that."

Matt said, "So you're going to make a bloodhound device, eh? How will it know which one you are and which is the other guy since you're identical?"

'Hmm. That's a good question, Matt. There must be a difference between us that I can home in on. I'm glad you asked that question. Thanks, Matt."

Matt beamed and walked over to Susie. "See, I can be helpful sometimes," he said, standing as close as he could to Susie without knocking her over.

"I never doubted that, Matt," Susie said, stepping sideways and away from Matt.

"So, did you want to go out with the smart guy tonight and grab some burgers?"

Susie thought about it, but her facial expression didn't make it appear that a positive answer was coming until Matt said, "I'll let you try my glass."

"Now that makes it interesting," Susie laughed. "I wanted to see if I could get that thing to make a milkshake from water."

"Never thought about that," Matt said. "Shall we go and give it a try?"

Matt held out his arm, and Susie intertwined hers. They walked out, Matt turning to Andrew and giving the thumbs up, Susie looking at Julie and Kota and rolling her eyes.

Kota asked, "Is there anything I can do to help Mr. B?"

"Not that I can think of, but thanks for asking. I just need to get on this and see where this other Andrew has gone and what he's up to."

"Okay," Kota said. "See you soon, Mrs. B."

"Bye, Kota," Julie said. "Thank you for coming over on such short notice."

"Did you call them all over?" Andrew asked, wrapping his arms around Julie.

"I thought maybe you could use some backup," Julie smiled.

"You think of everything. Thank you," Andrew said, kissing his wife.

"Now get to work on your tracker thing before this other Andrew starts causing trouble."

"Yes, Ma'am," Andrew teased, saluting.

Julie went into the house and Andrew started working. He felt good about this and he could block anything bad this guy would do. "Now, where did I put my notebook?" Andrew said to himself, realizing that many things besides his notebook seemed missing.

CHAPTER 22

One Step Forward

Andrew struggled throughout the weekend building his tracker device. Things were not where he always kept them, and he thought he knew now what the hide-and-seek portion of the game was. Somehow, Andrew 2 was hiding all of his important things, moving them from their normal homes and putting them somewhere else. Then, one thing he couldn't figure out was how Andrew 2 was doing it. No one ever saw him, and no one saw anything move.

When he went to work Monday morning, he thought about it and didn't hear the beeping sound when he swiped his name tag through the time clock reader. While preparing his paperwork, the personnel manager appeared and approached Andrew.

"Andrew!" Bill said. "How are you? What brings you in today?" Bill was smiling but serious.

"Hey, Bill. Same thing as every Monday," Andrew

replied. "Work."

Bill looked at Andrew for an uncomfortably long time without saying a word. Then Bill asked, "Can you come with me for a moment, Andrew?"

"Sure," Andrew said, wondering what was going on. He followed Bill up the stairs to the manager's offices and stood while Bill went through some papers on his desk.

"Ah, here it is," Bill said, picking up a paper. "Did you come in over the weekend and complete this request?" Bill handed the paper to Andrew.

Andrew read through the papers, and the comments and signatures certainly looked like his handwriting. Still, he had no recollection of filling out any such paper. He looked at the top and saw that it was a request for transfer. Andrew looked through the paperwork again and saw that the request was to move to the weekend shift, three, twelve hour shifts. "I certainly don't recall filing this out, Bill, and I don't want to change shifts. I love my weekends."

Bill looked at Andrew and scowled. "Andrew, it's tough to fill positions in this warehouse, so I'll let you stay on weekdays. Please don't repeat this, or you might lose your job."

"Yes, sir," Andrew said and flew back down the stairs to resume working. *This is going a little too far*, Andrew thought, and he resolved to do something about it when he got home.

As angry as Andrew was when he got home, it was nothing compared to what he was about to encounter from

Julie when he walked into the house.

He didn't even have time to close the front door before Julie yelled at him.

"What did you spend all of our money on?" Julie yelled.

"I don't know what you're talking about," Andrew said.

"Our money," Julie said. "All of our money in the bank is gone—every dime. You and I are the only ones who can access the account, and I hadn't touched it until I checked our balance today. So I'll ask you again, where did our money go?"

Julie was almost in tears.

Andrew walked over to hold her, but she pulled away. "Julie, we aren't the only ones with access to our accounts."

Julie looked at Andrew. Her eyes grew wide. "You're not telling me that the other Andrew did this?"

"He almost got me fired today at work. I need to find him and put a stop to this."

"But how will you do that?" Julie asked, beginning to sob. "He just seems to come and go whenever he wants. If you get too close, he just pushes that stupid button on his belt and disappears."

"The button on his belt," Andrew said. "That's it! I know how to get rid of him. Call Matt and Susie over. I might need that backup you were talking about."

"Are you going to be able to get our money back?

Andrew, we'll be in big trouble if we're broke until your next paycheck. We need groceries, and we have bills that need to be paid and…"

Andrew put his index finger on her lips. "Everything is going to be okay. Please go call, and all of you meet me in the garage."

Andrew ran out to the garage and hooked up what he had been working on all weekend. He turned on the circuits and put the mask on his face. It looked a lot like a welder's mask, but Andrew could see residual time displacement images on the small screen inside the mask.

Julie came into the garage, followed by Matt and Susie.

"Did you find him, buddy?" Matt asked.

"Still looking, Matt. I think I know where he is. Hold on, guys."

Andrew turned back to his workbench and turned on another device. A large glowing light pulsed into the garage. Almost instantly, Andrew 2 appeared. He looked around and began to clap.

"I figured you'd find a way to contact me and bring me back," Andrew 2 said. "I take it you've come to your senses?"

Susie stepped forward. "He's always had good sense. You're the one who needs some sense knocked into him."

"Wow, Susie," Andrew 2 said. "I always thought that you were the one with the smarts. Guess I was mistaken."

Susie looked like she was about to smack Andrew 2 when Andrew walked over to Julie and whispered something. She nodded and took Susie's arm. "Andrew has made a decision," she said. "Let's let him talk."

Susie wanted to pick something up and throw it but resisted the urge.

Andrew walked over to Andrew 2. "I've been thinking a lot about what you said, and I agree. It's time I stop working on these ridiculous inventions and be there for my family."

"Is this some kind of trick?" Andrew 2 asked suspiciously.

"No trick. Not at all. In fact, I'll show you."

Andrew picked up a piece of paper. "I'll start with this," Andrew said. He reached over to the workbench and grabbed a lighter.

"What is that?" Andrew 2 asked.

"Just notes," Andrew said.

"Hey, buddy," Matt said, "you're not really going to burn your notes, are you?"

"I've made my decision, Matt," Andrew said. "You'll understand as I explain."

Andrew turned back toward Andrew 2. "The way you snuck around really made me think about things."

"Snuck around?" Andrew 2 asked. "I didn't sneak

around. I just made sure that I was around a few minutes before and after you were going to do things. Since I'm you, I know where you kept all of your notes and all of your equipment. I would just move things to places I knew you wouldn't look when I knew you'd be looking for them."

"That was brilliant!" Andrew said. "And how you messed with my job and the bank account was truly genius. That's how I knew that you were much smarter than I."

"I'm glad you could see that," Andrew 2 said proudly.

"I realized that you had raided my lab before as well," Andrew said.

"Oh no," Andrew 2 said. "I had never been here before the day I wanted to destroy the POD."

Andrew lit the lighter. "Not in this time. I'm talking about the future. When you landed the POD when I wasn't there, you went through the lab and found something. The belt."

"Oh, that," Andrew 2 said nervously. "It was just something I stumbled across."

"I think," Andrew continued, "that you found my notes and then found the prototype. I think that because when I met my future self in the distant future, he didn't use the belt. That made me think that perhaps it had been stolen, and I had to devise something else."

Andrew 2 started to fidget. "I didn't realize that you could be a good detective. Bravo."

"I realized when we first talked that you weren't entirely me. When talking about Julie and Stephanie, you kept referring to them as 'my' family and not ours." Andrew lit the corner of the paper. It started to burn slowly. "It dawned on me that the belt was the key to all this. It wasn't the hiccup in time. The belt kept you in the fluid stream of time and allowed you to remain as an individual."

Andrew 2 started sweating. "What are you doing? What have you done? What is on that paper?"

"Oh, this?" Andrew held up the paper that was now about halfway gone. "This has the plans for the belt mag-trans device. I have to tell you, I was really upset about having to do this, but much later, I'll invent something else."

"Something else?" Andrew 2 was beginning to fade.

"Much later. Until then, and because of you," Andrew stepped up and spoke in Andrew 2's face, just inches away. He emphasized each word, "I will never invent the belt."

With that, he dropped the paper on the floor, and it burned its last little bit.

When Andrew looked up, Andrew 2 was gone. He turned to the others, who were staring at the empty spot that Andrew 2 had occupied.

"Did he push the button on his belt?" Andrew asked everyone standing there. "I watched the paper to make sure it burned completely and didn't see."

He looked at Susie, who started to laugh but turned her

head. Then he looked at Julie, who was trying not to laugh and turned away from Andrew's stare. Then he looked at Matt, who looked back at him and said, "Don't look at me. I was watching the little fire."

Andrew turned back toward Julie. "I need to know if he touched the button on his belt before disappearing!"

Julie regained her composure and wiped her eyes. "I'm sorry, sweetheart," she said. "We watched him as the paper burned, and you talked to him. When you looked down at the paper, the belt vanished, and he was grasping madly at his pants, trying to keep them from falling down."

Both girls started laughing madly again. As their laughter subsided, Julie asked Andrew, "So what are we going to do about the money?"

Andrew said, "I'm guessing that if you check the account, it's all back. When I made the conscious decision not to invent the belt device, Andrew 2 vanished, and it became like he was never here. Because I never created the belt, he had no way to come back to the proper time, and he became an echo in time!"

"Thank goodness," Julie said. "I want to run and just make sure by looking up our account online. Who's up for some lemonade?"

Matt was the first to reach the door and was followed by the others.

The whisper of voices could be heard in the still of the empty garage. "It's time, and all is ready. Let him go into the future a few more times, and then make sure he comes here. I want his technology to take me to earth!"

CHAPTER 23

Where No Living Being Goes

There are times in people's lives when they learn exactly what they're made of. These are the times when you don't think you can go on or when you don't think you'll make it through. These are the times when you pray for strength, even if you're not usually a praying person. These are the times when you know that if you give up, you'll never come back, you'll never go on, and you'll cease to live. Your will is gone, and you accept the end. This was one of those times. ~ Andrew Barton

The project that Andrew thought would only take a week took much longer than that. Every night, he would sequester himself in the garage. Julie and all of Andrew's friends who stopped by heard the hammering, the hiss of the welding torch, and the occasional expletive when Andrew hit his thumb with the hammer.

Finally, the day came, and he emerged from the garage with a smile and excitement. "Julie!" he ran through the house, calling for his wife. "Julie! I'm done. You've got to come see it."

Julie stepped out of the bathroom and smiled. "Goodness, Andrew. Life goes on outside the garage, and some of us have to use the bathroom occasionally. What are you yelling about?"

Andrew ran up to her, grabbed her hands, and started to dance around the room with her. "You're going to love this!" he said, as giddy as she had ever seen him. "Come on!"

With that, Andrew led her quickly down the stairs, through the kitchen, and out to the garage. He stood behind her and waited for her reaction.

The gasp that she uttered was more than enough for Andrew. "Isn't it beautiful?" he asked.

"Is that your POD?" Julie asked while slowly walking over to the large object in the garage. She looked with disbelief at the new shiny metal exterior. She noticed the cylinders secured to the outside of the oval-shaped POD. Andrew ran over and waved his hand over a section of the POD. As he did, an opening formed on the side of the structure.

Julie's mouth dropped. "This is just like what you told me about from your visit to the future."

"Oh, just wait," Andrew said excitedly. "I want you to see inside!"

Andrew led Julie inside the POD. She saw six seats along the wall and a seventh at a control panel. The control panel was amazing, with numerous computer screens and joysticks. Julie continued to look around in astonishment. "Andrew," she said, "this is all amazing! I can't believe you did this. I don't usually question things, but where did you get the money to do all of this? It must have cost a fortune! We really can't afford it."

She turned to Andrew, who was smiling. "It didn't cost us a dime," he said.

"How can that be?" she asked. "Did you find a way in the future to make things appear out of thin air, like Matt's glass?"

"Not at all," Andrew said. "I, we, have an investor."

Julie, again, looked astonished. "I thought you didn't want to tell anyone about this?"

"I didn't want to tell anyone, in this time, about this," Andrew said. "I went back to the future to get more information about the door system, and while I was there, I met this businessperson. I told him what I wanted to do, and he wanted to help. Because the currency in the future would be suspect here, he gave me gold to cash in and use to buy the supplies I needed. He's not expecting payment back because he said he'll get it back anyway. Pretty amazing, huh?"

His words trailed off as he saw Julie staring at him in disbelief. "I'm sorry, Andrew, but I don't understand this. Maybe it makes sense to you, but to me, it all sounds a little crazy. You know that I'm your biggest supporter, but think about what you're saying. This businessperson must want something in return for his investment. Did he say anything about what he might expect from you to repay his kindness?"

Andrew looked hurt but then thought about what Julie was saying. "Well, I guess he did say something. He said that I would be able to help him out soon enough. He knew that I was coming back to this time and had no assurances that I would ever be back, so I'm not sure what that meant."

Julie hugged Andrew and said, "Well, we won't worry about it now. You have assembled an amazing machine, and I can't wait to see what it can do."

"You won't have to wait," Andrew said. "Let's all go someplace this weekend. You, me, Matt and Susie. There's plenty of room,"

Julie started to feel some excitement at what Andrew was saying. "Where would we go? Anywhere in the world? Anywhere in time?"

"Well, we probably could," Andrew said with a sly grin, "but I was thinking about someplace that none of us would ever expect. Let's go into space and really see the world. The whole world!"

Julie jumped up and down like a little kid. "Oh, Andrew! That would be amazing! Can we take Stephanie?"

Andrew became serious for the first time. "I thought we could have Kota watch her, and it could just be us. We'll be back in a short time. In fact, we should be back within seconds of when we leave, so it won't be like we even left at all."

Julie looked disappointed at first but then smiled. "How long will we be gone?"

"It will feel like a few hours to us, but to people here, it will only seem like a few seconds."

Julie bubbled, "Okay then. Let's do it! I'll call Susie and Matt to come over, then I'll call Kota."

Andrew laughed. "Okay, okay. Before you do, however, I want to give you this." Andrew pulled a ring out of his pocket and handed it to her. "Oh, Andrew. You're asking me to marry you. Again?"

"This ring is used to open the POD," he laughed. "I'll show you how it works. I want you to have it, just in case you need to ever get inside."

"Why would I need to get inside without you?" she

asked.

"I just want you to have it," he replied.

Julie shrugged and put the ring on. Andrew stepped out of the POD and helped Julie out. He showed her how the ring worked and how it would open the door. He then showed her how to use it to open the door with a delayed-time lock. After a couple of tries, she was able to make the door appear and seal it up again. She thought it was a waste of time but secretly appreciated that she could see Andrew anytime.

When Susie and Matt came over, Susie was as excited as Julie had been. Matt, on the other hand, took the attitude of being bored. "Again?" he said, "We're going on another trip? This is getting to be so old."

"Well then," Andrew said, "I guess you could always stay home, and we can tell you all about it once we return."

"You could do that," Matt said, "but then you wouldn't have my guidance, protection, and sense of humor. Like just now when I was only kidding about not wanting to go. You thought I was serious. That cracks me up!"

"I'm glad you want to go," Andrew said, smiling.

"This is so exciting, Andrew," Susie said. "Should we pack anything for our trip?"

"We should only be gone a few hours," Andrew assured her. "You shouldn't have to pack anything. In fact, we can all go out and celebrate as soon as we get home."

Everyone smiled, nodded, and climbed on board.

Andrew basked in the glories of the compliments and the wonder Matt and Susie expressed at the interior of the new POD.

"How can we see anything if we're stuck inside

without windows?" Matt asked.

"That's right! You haven't seen the additions to what I had before. See the big screen TV on the wall?"

All eyes turned to where Andrew pointed.

"Yeah," Matt said. "Are we going to watch a recording of something you had made to impress us?"

"No. Let's see what's playing now." He turned it on to show them the glorious inside of the garage. Everyone laughed.

Once the group was inside, Andrew said, "Everyone pick a seat and strap in." Each person eagerly did so, and even though they all had great faith in Andrew, they had a certain apprehension at what was to come. The unknown gnawed at their insides, but it was overshadowed by the excitement and adrenaline coursing through their bodies.

Andrew made the adjustments and flipped some switches. This caused the computer screens to light up and programs to run. He typed in a few commands and then turned to his eager guests. "Are you ready?" They all nodded. "Are you sure?" They looked at each other with the slightest bit of doubt at the question. Before anyone could voice his or her thoughts, however, Andrew said, "Then, hold on."

There was the slightest shutter in the POD. If senses hadn't been heightened, they might not have noticed it, but they did notice, causing everyone to jump slightly.

It was hushed until Matt said, "That doesn't look like the earth or our garage outside, buddy."

Andrew looked up at the view screen to see a dark sky. Stars were twinkling through a misty but thin fog. On the horizon, red spots appeared to be glowing on the ground. Andrew checked the outside conditions and said, "The temperature is 78 degrees Fahrenheit. It's an oxygen atmosphere, and it would seem that the ground we're on is stable, but this isn't Earth. I'll have the computers analyze the stars to see where we are."

"Maybe we should just go home," Julie said nervously.

"This could be the adventure of a lifetime! What do the rest of you think? Should we go back now, or do you want to explore what's out there?" Andrew was hopeful that everyone's curiosity was as great as his.

"The last time we went someplace, we ended up being celebrities. I say we stay." Matt said.

Susie shifted in her chair. "I guess staying for a while wouldn't be bad," she said. "I'm kind of curious to see where we are."

"Okay," Julie said. "I'll agree to stay, but only for a short while. We go back at the first sign of anything going wrong, Agreed?"

Everyone nodded, and Andrew smiled. He returned to the computer and entered the commands to compare the night sky to their original departure location. Just as he finished, there was a knocking on the side of the POD. It was a timid knock but loud enough that they all heard.

Matt unbuckled his seatbelt and jumped to where the door should be. "I'll get it," he said, searching for the door.

"Do you think we should open it?" Julie said cautiously.

"Why not?" Matt said. "They had the courtesy to knock; we should have the courtesy to answer. Toss me that door ring of yours, buddy."

Andrew stood up and walked over to the door. "I don't want to lose this, Matt," Andrew said, "so I think it's going to stay put on my finger."

Andrew walked over to the port and waved his ring over the receiver. The door opened, and warm, humid air rushed in. It had a sulfur smell, and Andrew, along with everyone else, wrinkled their noses. When the opening was completed, Matt ran over and stuck his head out the door to look around. As he did, a young woman ran from around the side of the POD and almost ran into Matt's protruding form.

"Sir," she said, breathing hard, "you must come with me. The sun will be up in a few hours, and you won't be safe here."

Matt found the young woman very attractive, and he was ready to not only run away with her but stay with her as well. He didn't speak and lost his thoughts, staring at her.

"Sir?" she said. "Do you understand me?"

"Oh yes," Matt said dreamily. "Probably much better than you'll ever know."

Andrew came to the opening and looked out. "Hello," he said. "My name is Andrew, and my love-struck friend here is Matt. We won't be staying long."

"Sir," the woman said, looking around. "You really don't understand. Let me take you to the castle where you'll be safe until the sun sets again. Our king is eager to meet you."

By this time, both Susie and Julie had left the comfort of their seats and joined the others in the doorway. "You wanted adventure," Julie said. "Maybe we should go with her. She seems sincere."

Whatever doubts Julie had, she kept to herself, but deep inside, she didn't like or trust this woman.

Andrew looked around and felt Julie's discomfort. He

was about to decline when Matt hopped out of the POD and said, "Yeah, we'll go. The king, huh? He wants to meet us? Cool."

Susie shrugged and stepped out of the POD as well.

"I don't like the feel of this," Julie said. "How did the king know we were here? We just arrived, and without fanfare, I would guess."

"I don't know," Andrew said, "but I suspect we'll find out. We can't just let our friends go off by themselves."

Julie reluctantly stepped out, followed by Andrew, who put his hand in hers as they walked. "I'm sure we'll be fine," he assured her, but she wasn't assured. She was far from it. Her intuition told her that something terrible was going to happen. Something horrible.

As the door sealed and they walked away, a beeping noise from inside the POD sounded, unheard by Andrew or anyone else who had left the safety of the POD. The message window on the computer screen read, "Starfield verified. Cannot coordinate location. You've gone too far out. Imperative you begin the return sequence to go back home immediately."

CHAPTER 24

What the King Wants

The young woman walked quickly along a well-worn path. Although it was dark, Andrew thought the land seemed very smooth, lacking vegetation. The sky on the horizon was beginning to lighten, and he noticed that this young woman, who had never offered her name, continually glanced toward that direction. Andrew looked again and saw that the red glowing spots were increasing in number and intensity where the ground met the sky.

"We have to hurry," the young woman said. "We're almost there."

They rounded a large boulder and came to an opening. "Quickly. In here," she said, ducking into the cave.

Matt eagerly followed. Susie grumbled but went inside. Andrew stopped for a moment and looked back at the horizon. It looked as if the sun would peak over the top at any moment. He was still holding Julie's hand and noticed their palms were sweaty.

"Hurry," the young woman said, "the sun is almost up!"

Andrew and Julie stepped inside. Immediately, a large boulder rolled into place, blocking any escape. It was dark. Andrew noticed that the walls were glowing a soft red glow, which grew in intensity until the inside of the cave was visible. "This way," the young woman said, leading them to an alcove in the wall. Once inside, an elevator-like mechanism kicked in, and they began to descend slowly to another level. As they slowly dropped into the Earth, Andrew asked, "Do you have a name, young woman?"

"I do, sir," the young woman replied without looking at Andrew. "They call me Naamah."

"That's an interesting name," he replied.

"It is a name," she said distractedly. "Each of us has one which is decreed before heaven prior to our birth. Mine is no more interesting than yours, Andrew. It is simply different than yours. Although many people have the same names, each name is slightly different and declared differently before heaven."

"So your people believe in heaven?" Andrew asked.

"We not only believe in it, we know it is real," she said. "Unlike your people who have to speculate, we know."

"How do you know, Naamah?"

"The king will explain all of this and more to you."

As Naamah said this, the door opened into a well-lit rock walled room. People mulled around and stopped when they saw the doors open. Susie leaned over to Julie and whispered, "Looks like these people aren't very happy. No one is smiling at all. They all look like they've given up."

Julie looked around and felt sadness. These people,

each one, looked as if they had lost everything. A bell started to ring, and they all walked as if on cue toward various openings in the walls.

Naamah said, "I will take you to see the king now. He is expecting you."

Julie said, "How is it that the king knows we're here?"

"The king knows everything. He has told us for months that you would be arriving and will greatly help him. I was privileged to be the one chosen to greet you upon your arrival. I will be rewarded. Please come this way."

Julie looked at Andrew as Naamah walked away. "How are we going to help the king?"

"Beats me," Andrew said, "but if I can help someone in need, then I'll do what I can."

They walked for what seemed to be fifteen minutes. The rocky walls suddenly came to an end, and they entered into a large reception area. The floors were marble. Large chandeliers hung from the ceiling. Statues adorned the walls. Matt looked around and said, "Now, this is what I call a royal welcome!"

They continued to walk across the grand room until they came to large, double doors. Naamah stopped and said, "Please wait here. I will announce you to the king."

Everyone had noticed how attractive this woman was, and each person, both men and women, found themselves in some way attracted to her. When she walked through the doorway and closed the door behind her, it was like an emotional light had gone out.

At that moment, no one knew what to say. There was some internal embarrassment at the thought, but no one wanted to be the first except Matt. He always seemed to speak what others only thought.

"Wow, did anyone else feel that? It was almost like having a first kiss without the kiss."

Even with that introduction, no one else said anything. The silence was broken when the large doors once again opened. A man in his mid-forties with dark hair and a very expensive looking suit walked through the doors. His smile was broad, and he was very handsome. He stuck out his hand and walked straight over to Andrew.

"Mr. Andrew Barton! I am so happy to finally meet you in person. I was beginning to wonder if I would ever have this opportunity, yet here you are. I see that you brought your closest friends with you as well."

He turned to Julie and again stuck out his hand, only this time he took her hand gently, held it up to his mouth, and softly kissed the back of it without taking his eyes off of her.

"Julie Barton," he said softly, "I feel like I have known you for years. Your very thoughts surround me daily, and I think about your ability to remain faithful to such a man as this, Andrew. You are truly blessed with patience." He glanced at Andrew and said, "No offense, sir. I speak the truth as I see it."

He released Julie's hand and winked at her blushing face. "Truth sometimes makes one blush when it's revealed openly." He walked over to Matt and grabbed his hand. "Matt Berman, as I live and breathe! What an amazing man you are. You shall be the toast of the town here. So many people in my kingdom wish they could be you. It's amazing how innocent you are, yet you can still make the most interesting mistakes. My young friend, you shall find the fame you've always wanted here. I shall see to that!"

He looked at Susie, and as he slowly let go of Matt's hand, he said, "Susie Montgomery. The single most sought after part of Mr. Berman's life." He walked over, took her hand, and kissed it like he had Julie's. "I know where your heart lies. Shall I announce it in the presence of these fine people? No? Well, since I do indeed know your heart, we will keep it our little secret, yes? You shall come in handy while you're here, my dear."

"Now, Mr. Barton," the king said, turning toward Andrew. "I sense that you're wondering why I brought you here."

"Why you brought me here? I'm sure you didn't bring me here, but it was an error or miscalculation that I ended up here, and I'm hoping that we can help you with whatever it is you need and be on our way."

The king laughed an infectious laugh. After a minute of laughing, the king daubed his eyes. "Oh my, that is humorous," he said. "No, no. Mr. Barton. There was no miscalculation. Not at all. I knew you were coming. Look carefully at me. Do you not recognize me?"

Andrew looked carefully at the king and then realized who he was. "You're the investor that gave me the gold to make improvements on the POD."

"Yes, yes," the king said, smiling. "Very good. Now, your next question would be, are we then in the future where you and I met? The answer to that is no. I have the ability to influence people on Earth for short periods of time. Very short periods. I also have the ability to take on the appearance of anyone I choose. An amazing ability, to say the least. I do, however, always have many agents on the Earth. They help me from a distance. Now that you have arrived, Mr. Barton, with your amazing POD device, you will be able to help me return to Earth, where I will be free of this planet they call my kingdom and will be able to once again rule over mankind as I was meant to do from the beginning."

Andrew listened to what he thought were ravings from a tortured soul. "I'm not really sure I can help you with that. As far as I know from visiting the future, there is no king of the Earth."

"Mr. Barton," the king said, "as you know, timelines can change. They are fluid, and like all fluids, they can be rerouted in several ways. What you have seen in your future is not set in stone."

"I really think we need to get back to my POD now. I need to check on some programming that I set before we left, so if you would be so kind as to show us the way out, I'd be very appreciative."

The king smiled at Andrew. "Would you like to go back to your POD? Well, please let me personally show you to the exit door."

The king started walking and arrived at another elevator across the room. He stepped inside and motioned to the others to follow. Reluctantly, they all filed in. "You don't have to be so timid," the king said. "You have my solemn word that I will not hurt any of you."

Somehow, his "word" didn't seem to carry much weight. While he seemed likable enough and he hadn't hurt them or held them against their will, there was something untrustworthy about the King. The elevator made its way slowly upward. The farther up it went, the hotter it became. Soon, they stopped, but the doors didn't open.

The king said, "We have reached the surface, and you

are free to go if you want. Please note, however, that the sun has come up, and as Naamah mentioned, it's not very pleasant when the sun is up. I will leave it up to you. It's a little warm, by the way."

The doors opened slowly, and the group was assaulted by a blast of heat unlike any they had ever felt. But it wasn't the heat that made them all stop in their tracks. What they saw was horrific. They saw hundreds of thousands of people crowded together in groups on small, solid plots of land. Between the land masses were rivers of lava lapping at the edges of the tiny islands. Every now and again, a person would fall off; their screams were sickening, and they would be pulled back up to the island by those still standing on it. Even though they would be burning and smoldering, they were still alive and would stand next to those on the island, gazing off at a bright oval light in the distance.

Matt asked, "What is the glowing oval across the way they're all staring at?"

The king answered, "That's the gateway to heaven."

Julie trembled.

"Do you have a question for me, Julie?" the king asked, not looking at her.

"You never told us your name," she said.

"I have many," he calmly replied. "I'm not sure exactly which one is in vogue now. I believe that Lucifer is the most common, but you can call me what you'd like. And to answer the question on your mind, Mr. Barton, the name of this planet is Hades. Be pleased, Mr. Berman. I promised that you would enjoy great fame. You and your party are the first living beings to visit Hell."

CHAPTER 25

The Plan

Lucifer took them back to the main reception room, where they filed out. They felt almost as downtrodden as the people they had seen earlier that morning. Andrew was well aware at this point that Lucifer knew what they were thinking, so he tried to think only generic thoughts. Maybe he should think thoughts that he knew Lucifer would expect him to believe, so he tried to think about giving in and letting him have what he wanted.

"I've had some rooms prepared for you to stay until the sun goes down," he told them. "You'll be very comfortable here. Much more comfortable than my permanent guests. Most of them brought this on themselves during their existence on Earth. You four, however, would have never seen this place. You all have good hearts, except Matt."

Matt looked at him questioningly.

"You have the simple heart of a child and will your

entire life. There's nothing I could ever do to get you."

"What about the rest of us," Andrew asked. "Could you 'get' us?"

Lucifer sighed. "My talent is simple. I know what you think you want and what you feel. I know this about every person who has ever existed. I know your weaknesses and your desires. Many people have desires that don't fit their universe's laws."

"What do you mean?" Matt asked.

"Ah, I see you need some explanation," Lucifer said. "Mr. Barton understands. He's traveled to an alternate dimension where his laws are foreign to those who live there. You understand, don't you, Mr. Barton?"

Andrew nodded and thought about his brief visit to the other dimension in weeks past.

"You see, Mr. Berman, every dimension has different good and evil laws, much like the difference between many laws in your Europe and your United States. I'll give you a simple example. In the United States, it's against the law for anyone under the age of 21 to consume alcoholic beverages. In Europe, families can drink wine together no matter what their age. In the United States, alcohol is one of my biggest temptations and evils. It's so much easier to get into the minds of younger people, especially when they've been drinking, and tempt them to do things they normally wouldn't do. I see their desires, their lusts, and their jealousies. I can influence them to do what they aren't supposed to do, and they do it. I influence people to observe monogamy in other dimensions, like the one Mr. Barton visited. It's frowned upon there, and many other things that your society would find acceptable. There are countless dimensions, and each one is different according to their laws of good and evil. Earth, in the dimension you're from, is the most fun and the easiest to rule. Every day, people find new ways to make the unacceptable acceptable. Can you imagine a ruler who would allow anything pleasurable to be legal? That's why I want to go there and physically be there. In your world, I have great power. Here, I'm more or less a gatekeeper, and I have my agents to touch the minds of those who are less pure and weak on Earth. I miss being able to do that myself, and you, Mr. Barton, will help me get back and fulfill my desire."

"I guess I really don't have a choice, do I?" Andrew replied.

"Andrew," Julie said quietly, "we've already been here for several hours. What about Stephanie? What about Kota? What will they do if we're here until the sun sets again? I don't even know how long a day is here."

"Interestingly enough, Mrs. Barton," Lucifer said, "there is no time here. I decide when the sun will rise and set. This place is in a bubble. One of many that you would refer to as eternity. When Andrew travels, he mainly only travels in a straight line, forward and backward. When he enters his POD, he essentially enters eternity and can actually travel in any direction. When he crossed over into the other dimension, the one that causes you great suspicion and jealousy to this day, he went a little sideways without knowing it. Imagine a sphere. If you are in the center of that sphere, you have countless ways that you could go to reach the edge. It's the same when Andrew enters his POD. Right now, however, he only thinks in a linear plane. Forward and backward. There is so much more that he could explore. When he travels unprotected and enters that realm of eternity, it's effortless for me to reach out and guide his POD here. Fortunately for me, he tried again without considering the protection issue."

Julie glared at Andrew. "What? I didn't know," Andrew said defensively.

"Maybe if you had taken more time to look into how it all worked and considered this, we wouldn't be here right now," Julie snapped.

Lucifer broke in. "This is what I'm talking about! I could make this argument go on forever. I could make both of you miserable with each other, but you still love each other so much that you'd never consider leaving the other. It would be your living hell. How I miss seeing that," he sighed.

Julie immediately turned to Andrew and said, "I'm sorry, sweetheart. It wasn't your fault."

"Disgusting," Lucifer said. "If you didn't know what I was thinking, you never would have apologized." He looked over across the room where Naamah had just entered. "Show them to their rooms and make sure that they are comfortable. I'll leave when the sun sets at the end of the day."

"Yes, sir," she said. "Follow me."

The two rooms were luxurious and had almost everything they could ask for. Food and drink, movies, beds, showers, and anything else they might want. Although they had all these comforts, they couldn't do anything but think about their predicament. Andrew had a plan in the back of his mind, but he didn't dare say it out loud or think of it too openly. He would wait until the right time before it came to the surface. The words of his older self continued to haunt him, and he wondered if this was the trial he would have to endure.

CHAPTER 26

The Battle

Andrew wanted to pace, but he knew that doing so would cause him to start thinking, and that was the last thing he wanted to do. Thinking would be like broadcasting his every move to Lucifer. It was hard enough with Julie asking him questions.

"What are we going to do?" Julie asked.

"We're going to see what happens," Andrew answered.

"How can you say that?" she growled. "You're just going to sit back and wait until he's in the POD and on his way to Earth?"

"Nope. I'm going to wait and see what happens," Andrew said, lying on the bed and placing his hands behind his head.

"We need to come up with a plan," Julie said.

"No, we don't," Andrew replied.

Julie was having trouble believing what she was hearing. In all the time she had known him, she had never known Andrew to be a quitter or give up. But now it looked as if he was headed in that direction.

Julie thought about getting Matt and Susie from the next room and making a plan without Andrew. Still, she was more curious about why Andrew acted the way he was.

"Why don't you want to at least devise some kind of plan?" Julie asked.

"I don't think it would be a good idea. There's no way we can get out during the day, and Lucifer will probably escort us to the POD when it gets dark, so let's just see what happens," Andrew insisted.

Just as Julie was about to tell Andrew his attitude was hopeless, Matt and Susie walked into the room. "Hey, buddy," Matt said. "These are great rooms! Too bad there's not a window with a view. I'd even settle for a skylight."

"You probably know that room better than anyone," Susie complained. "All you did from the time we walked through the door was explore every inch of it. I'm amazed that you didn't find a secret escape route."

"I did," Matt said. "Didn't you hear me say that? You were probably too involved in your own thoughts."

"What!" Both Julie and Susie responded at the same time.

"Matt looked up from being distracted and held up his hands to protect himself, cringing slightly. "Whoa, whoa. I was only joking."

Both of the girls looked incredibly angry and disappointed. Matt thought it best to return to his room and look for a way out. Since everyone seemed to be sulking, that's what he did. He snuck out and slipped back into his room, looking at every crack and seam that could possibly be a secret passageway.

Andrew sat up on the edge of the bed, and Susie plopped down on the other side. Julie looked up and asked, "Why is it, Andrew Barton, that you have no interest in coming up with a way to get us out of here? What is going on in that brain of yours?"

Andrew looked up. "Julie, Lucifer said that he could read our minds. No, wait. He never really said that. He implied that he could by saying he knew we were thinking certain things." Andrew stood and paced. "I'm pretty sure he never really said he could read our minds. He said, 'I know what you're thinking.'" Andrew hit himself in the forehead. "I'm so stupid! All this time, I thought that if I thought too hard about something, he would know what I was thinking. I don't remember what he said for sure, and maybe he just made me think he could read my mind. This changes everything. Let's start planning. Where's Matt? He should be in on this, too."

"He was here the last time I looked," Susie said, looking around. "Maybe he went back to our room."

The three entered the room next door, where Matt and Susie stayed. When they walked in, the room was empty.

"Matt?" Susie called.

A muffled sound came from the far side of the room. The noise continued as they walked closer and closer to where the sound was emanating.

"It seems to be coming from over here," Andrew said, standing by the large flat-screen TV. The women joined him, and they all agreed.

"Matt?" Susie yelled. "Are you in here somewhere?"

The muffled voice sounded again. "Sounds like Matt's telling us to turn on the TV," Julie said. They looked around for a button of some type to press, but none could be found.

Andrew looked around the table just below the TV and found what looked like a remote. Numerous buttons adorned the cylindrical object, but one red one stuck out. "I'm going to try this one," he announced, pushing the button.

Without delay, the large screen lit up. Matt appeared, pressing his face to the screen. "Hey, buddy," Matt said. "Look at me, I'm on TV. Well, I'm not really on TV. I'm in TV. I'm unsure how I got here, but maybe you could help me get out?"

Susie approached the TV and put her face up against the screen. "Oh, Matt," she said. "If only you hadn't got yourself into this predicament. I wanted so much to kiss you." She put her lips on the TV screen and puckered. Matt tried desperately to return the kiss but only felt the cold glass.

"Wait!" Matt said. "Just hold that thought and get me out of here! I can help you. Just don't forget that you wanted to do this."

"I'm not sure I'll be in the mood by the time that happens, Matt," Susie sighed.

Just as she started to chuckle, they all heard a noise in the room and turned to see Naamah walking in.

"I came to see if there was anything that any of you needed," she said, looking at the screen they had all gathered around. "I see that Mr. Berman was exploring."

Andrew stepped forward and said, "Yeah. He does that a lot. Is there any way that you can help us with this? Can you get him out of the TV?"

"Of course," she said and walked over to the table where Andrew had placed the remote. "This device, as you may have surmised, controls the viewer. This isn't a TV as you think of them. As you learned, this planet is outside the normal realm of time and dwells in eternity. If you compared the time here to your time on earth, ours is much slower than yours. One day here is the same as many days on earth. This control stick opens the portal to a place outside that eternity so that time resumes for the person inside. Those dead souls who come here are often, how shall I say it, rebellious. They feel that they don't belong here. Those who cause trouble are placed in this environment where they can feel the effects of age without dying, growing extremely old, and feeling the aches and pains of life. Feeling tired and helpless. Once the new residents have reached the point where they feel they can no longer resist, they are brought back here."

Naamah pressed three buttons on the controller, and the "screen" fogged. As it did, Naamah said, "You may come out now, Mr. Berman."

Matt almost fell out of the screen and stayed on the floor, breathing heavily.

"He'll be fine after a little rest," Naamah said.

"Fine?" Matt said, huffing and puffing. "I feel like I just gained two hundred pounds. I can barely move and can't breathe very well. I could sure use a kiss." Matt glanced up at Susie, who shook her head.

"Nice try, Matt," she said.

Naamah looked at Matt and said, "I don't understand how it would help, however..." She knelt down and kissed Matt on the lips. He looked up dreamy-eyed, but Naamah only looked uninterested and bored.

Susie, on the other hand, bristled. She walked over to Matt and tried to help him up. She was joined by Andrew and

Julie. Susie shot Naamah a very dirty look as they placed Matt on the bed to rest.

Susie turned back to Naamah. "So what was all that about?"

"I can tell you're jealous, but that is my calling in life."

"What?" Susie said.

"Do you remember when I first led you down here and told you we all have names? That our names represent our station in life?" Naamah asked.

"I remember you saying that, yes," Andrew replied.

"I am a succubus. My name indicates that I seduce people, and I steal their health and their lives slowly. It's my nature and who I am," she said matter-of-factly. "If a man or a woman expresses a desire out of loneliness or lust, I can visit them in their dreams and eventually take on a physical form. Then I take their health, and eventually, I can steal their life."

"Fine profession," Susie hissed.

"An old and noble profession," Naamah replied. "I give most people comfort. I give others discomfort. I comforted Matt, and how I comforted him took comfort from you. This is what must have happened and this is who I am. There must be a balance in all things. I give comfort to one and cause misery to another. It's the way of the universe."

"And is that why you came here just now? To give Matt your comfort?" Susie was starting to steam.

"Not at all," Naamah said. "I came to help you get home without Lucifer going with you. He's needed here, and here is where he should stay."

There was stunned silence.

"How can you help us to get home? What can you do

to keep Lucifer here?" Andrew asked.

"When the time comes," Naamah said, "you must go home on your own. I considered trying to convince you that I should go with you, and I would have been very successful at it, but I don't have that much desire to go. I like living in eternal time. In the meantime, you need to devise a plan, and I will do whatever I can to help you."

Andrew realized something just said was the key to getting home and leaving Lucifer behind. He wasn't sure how or if it would work, but he couldn't think of any other way.

"I have an idea," he said to everyone, gathering them around to hear. He wasn't sure why he did that. It's what they always did in the movies. For some reason, everyone had to gather in a football-like huddle to discuss whatever plan they had come up with, so it seemed like the thing to do! The plan was pretty simple but had some risks. They all agreed to try it and go from there.

CHAPTER 27

Dancing With the Devil

For the remainder of the afternoon, the group rested in their rooms. Matt regained his strength and teased Susie about being jealous.

"I wasn't jealous," Susie said. "I was more worried about your well-being than anything."

"Thanks, Susie," he said, smiling broadly.

After what felt like an eternity, an alarm sounded, signaling the end of the day. There were sounds of people shuffling into the hallways. The sun was setting, and the day's torments were slowly ending. Matt and Susie moved into the room with Andrew and Julie.

"It must almost be time to go," Andrew said. "I wonder how long it takes for the surface to cool enough for us to walk to the POD?"

"It doesn't take long at all."

Andrew turned to see Lucifer walking into the room. "In fact, we'll be able to leave in a few minutes. Please make sure you have everything you need. Naamah will lead the way back, and I will bring up the rear. I beg your indulgence. I'll be back shortly. Then we can leave."

Lucifer turned and walked out of the room.

"Do you think he knows?" Matt asked Andrew in a low voice.

"I don't think so," Andrew replied. "It doesn't matter if he does, though. I'm sure it will work whether he knows or not."

Matt looked at Andrew, and for the first time since he started working with the POD, he could swear that he saw doubt in Matt's face.

Lucifer reentered the room. "Well, my friends. I don't know about you, but I'm ready to go." He took a deep breath through his nose. "I can almost smell the stale Earth air. Do all of you have what you need to get back home?" he asked.

No one replied, and Lucifer just shrugged.

"Follow Naamah," he said in a tone that indicated that this was more of an order than a request. When everyone hesitated momentarily, Lucifer's face reflected the anger of an eternity. The four could not only see but also feel the searing anger emitted from this man. They all quickly walked toward the door and the waiting Naamah.

"Follow me, please," Naamah said, opening the door and stepping through.

The procession looked like an African safari. Naamah was the guide, and everyone else followed in line.

"I'll lead," Matt said, hurrying to stand behind Naamah."

"Why don't you stand behind me, and I'll stand behind Naamah?" Susie said, gently taking Matt by the shoulders and moving him behind her.

"Are you sure?" Matt asked. "I really don't mind."

Susie glared at him, and Matt promptly quieted.

With Julie nestled between Andrew and Matt, Andrew and Lucifer brought up the rear.

They entered the doorway and began the steep ascent to the surface. Lucifer took a few steps toward Andrew and said just loud enough for him to hear, "I know that you have a plan to escape, Andrew, but it won't work. You'll die first, and then you'll be here with me forever!"

Andrew felt a shiver of fear run through his body but did his best to maintain his composure. He knew Lucifer was just trying to upset and cause him to give something away.

"I don't know what you're talking about," Andrew replied. "I intend to stay alive and live a very long life. Why would I want to escape without you? It doesn't make any sense."

"Virtue seldom makes sense, Mr. Barton," Lucifer chuckled.

"Better to be alive and not virtuous and able to do whatever makes me happy than dead and able to do nothing with your virtue intact," Andrew quipped.

Lucifer laughed loudly! Loudly enough, everyone stopped and turned to see what the joke was. Lucifer wiped his eyes and motioned for everyone to keep going. "Mr. Barton," he said, "when I am in charge of Earth and its people, I'll have to ensure you have a nice job by my side. I can use a good laugh from time to time."

Andrew felt like he was being offered the job of court jester. *The joke will be on you soon enough*, Andrew thought to himself, and he waited to see if there would be any reaction or repercussion. When none came, Andrew was sure that Lucifer could not read his mind, and he only speculated what people were thinking based on the responses to his statements!

It didn't seem to take as long to reach the surface as Andrew thought it should have. It honestly didn't surprise him as when he traveled home from a trip, it always seemed to take less time than it did to travel away to the destination.

When they exited to the surface, Andrew thought it felt like the summer nights he remembered from living in Maryland as a boy. It was hot and humid. Lightning flashed in the sky, and thunder rumbled. The wind picked up, and raindrops started to fall. As the land became increasingly wet, thick mud formed, making walking more challenging and making the trip slow quite a bit. Each step created a sucking motion as their boots were pulled from the ground.

Eventually, though, they arrived at the POD. Andrew's heart soared when he saw it, and he imagined that the others felt their freedom was just moments away!

The party walked up to the POD's side, where Andrew knew the door was hidden. He stopped and looked at the smooth surface.

"The time has come, Mr. Barton," Lucifer said in a surly voice. "Open the POD, and let's go."

Andrew started to lift his hand and then put it back down again. "No," he said defiantly.

Lucifer raised his eyebrows, but no one could see the action in the dark. "No?" he asked. "What part about you dying didn't you understand, Mr. Barton? Once you're dead, it wouldn't take me long to remove the ring from your finger and use it myself. I assure you that your death would not be pleasant either, but it doesn't need to be that way. Open the door, Mr. Barton!"

Andrew turned and walked about five feet from the POD, turned and looked at Lucifer, and said, "I have no intention of opening that door. Now, if you're going to kill me, then I guess it will happen. I suspect you wouldn't let me live once we arrived on Earth anyway. I could easily go back in time and change what happened so that I would never leave to come here, resulting in you never going to Earth. I do have one thought, though. One suggestion that could certainly change everything."

An extremely red-faced and angry Lucifer said, "And let me know, please, Mr. Barton, what that might be."

"This," Andrew said, pulling the remote from his room out of his pocket.

"Oh no, Mr. Barton," Lucifer chuckled. "I'm so scared. Please don't zap me with the remote!" Even though Lucifer mocked Andrew, he didn't know the plan's scope.

"I won't zap you. I promise." He pushed some buttons on the remote and tossed it to Julie. "Now!" he shouted. Julie caught the remote, and Julie, Matt, and Susie vanished.

Lucifer stared at where the group had stood. "What have you done?" he shouted to Andrew. Lucifer grabbed him by the shirt and pushed him into the mud. Andrew struggled to get up and move away from Lucifer toward the POD.

"I simply modified the remote to create a field around the one holding it. Once Julie caught it, she pushed the 'on' button, dropping them out of the eternity bubble. Essentially, they returned to the Earth's timeline, and their time sped up in relation to us. They are now safely in the POD and should be activating the auto-return sequence.

"Understand, Mr. Barton, if I don't leave here, you never will either." He picked up Andrew and threw him like a rag doll against the POD. Andrew felt the wind being knocked out of him. He stood unsteadily on his feet and faced his opponent again.

"I won't give up until I'm dead," he said to Lucifer.

"I can fix that, and then I'll enter your POD by whatever means necessary. He started toward Andrew with fierce anger in his eyes.

Inside the POD, Julie had turned off the remote device to bring time back in synch with the outside, hoping that Andrew might have a chance to escape and come inside. She knew that the plan was for them to leave without him, and it made her feel sick inside. A tear rolled down her cheek as Julie thought about it. "We can't just leave him," she cried.

An alarm blared inside, indicating the intruders had entered. "We don't have a choice," Matt said. "I just hope he knows what he's doing and that his plan works."

Matt silenced the alarm and found the auto-return icon on the desktop. He hesitated briefly and then pressed the icon on the screen. The countdown started. He hurried to his seat, strapped himself in, and waited.

Outside, the fight continued and seemed, in Andrew's mind, like it would never end. He would try to escape momentarily, and Lucifer would pick him up again and throw him against the POD. He felt bruised and broken each time and wondered if he would have the strength to get up again. As his body was slammed into the side of the steel-encased POD again, he fell to the ground. After the next slam, he realized he couldn't get up. Lucifer came over and picked him up by the throat. He lifted him into the air, choking the life from him. Andrew grabbed at Lucifer's hand, trying to loosen his grip.

"Let me into the POD," Lucifer demanded.

Lucifer loosened his grip just enough for Andrew to speak. "A little help here," he croaked. "Anytime now."

"There's no one here to help you," Lucifer said, grinning. "Goodbye to the mortal Mr. Barton. Soon, you'll be here for eternity, wishing you could go back and change the circumstances of your death. You'll see your wife and daughter every day through visions. You'll wish to help them but never be there for them. You'll watch them struggle and lament at your passing. You'll be miserable for all eternity!"

As he said this, he felt a hand on his shoulder. Surprised, he turned to see Naamah. She grabbed his face and kissed him passionately. The surprise caused him to drop Andrew.

Lucifer pushed her away. "You can't seduce me!" he yelled at her.

"Oh, but I can. I can seduce anyone. I've seduced angels and demons alike. She held his gaze, but Lucifer looked away and turned his fury toward Andrew. He picked him up and prepared to throw him for the final time against the POD. As he did, the POD started to glow slightly, and a gray oval formed, sucking the POD into its center. Lucifer screamed, "NO!" and, unable to stop his started motion, hurled Andrew into the oval as the POD vanished. Andrew's body was sucked into the oval and vanished as the oval collapsed and disappeared.

Lucifer stood breathing heavily in the ensuing silence. He could only hear the sound of the rain falling and the footsteps of Naamah running away. She knew that there was no place that she could hide. She also knew that there was nothing Lucifer could do to her and that he needed her to continue to do what she had always done to further his work. It would not be pleasant for a while, but eventually, things would return to normal. She also knew he would never forget this traitorous act. She wondered how unpleasant things would be for her until he accepted this event or found another opportunity. For now, she just wanted him to follow her and hoped Andrew would be alright.

CHAPTER 28

The Circle

We tend to believe our senses, provided we can verify what our senses are telling us. Sometimes, our minds can play tricks on us. Other times, the outside world can play tricks on our minds. Either way, we need to sort it out, and if we have done something wrong, we need to correct it as best we can. We don't always get a second chance, but when we do, grab it and do our best to set things right! ~ Andrew Barton

He remembered the fight and being thrown—the throw that sent him through the foggy oval back to this place. His mind reeled as he thought. He wasn't sure if the fight or the throwing had sent him here. And where was here?

The floor was cold and hard under his back. His head throbbed. He sat up and fought the darkening feeling of passing out. His body hurt. His joints hurt. Hurting was a good thing. At least if he hurt, he knew he was alive.

He wanted to open his eyes. Julie may be standing over him. Julie! He forced his swollen eyes open. Was Julie okay?

Had she, Matt, and Susie made it home?

Home.

He looked around and realized he was home in his garage. The memories of what had just transpired started to mingle with other memories. He had the feeling that something had exploded. Did it explode, or was it the shock of being drawn into the oval? He thought more. He felt as if he had been experimenting all day. Experimenting. No, he had been in Hades with Matt, Susie, and Julie. But where were they, and where was he? He looked around, and his eyes started to focus. His garage. He was home in his garage. Andrew knew that? He looked toward the garage door. Where was his POD? It wasn't there. Had Matt pressed the wrong button? Were his wife and friends lost somewhere in time and space? Why was he thinking about an explosion? Was that the first explosion? He had to guess. He wanted to pace, but the dried mud on the outside of his jeans also lined the inside. He thought it might be better to just sit. This morning. It had to be. It was this morning when everything was good, and time only meant that he might be late for something. Now, time has an entirely different meaning. It wasn't something on a clock. That was how we tracked it according to our understanding of it. Time was fluid. Time was a pliable fluid. This morning, it wasn't, however. Was it? This morning, everything was so much different. No! This morning was all at his command.

He wanted to look at the clock but knew what it would read. Still, being human, he looked anyway. 7:05. Just as before. Just as before, what? He weighed the possibility that he had gone back before it all happened. Had it really happened, or had he dreamt it? He hurt, and he was muddy. It had to have all been real. But why was he here now? Why did he have the beginning of conflicting memories? According to the clock, this morning was only 12 hours ago. According to his body, this morning was a few weeks ago. No, this morning was a few months ago. This morning, Andrew thought. What really happened this morning? Not the morning in his memory, but the morning of this day.

He sat up, wondering. The door from the garage to the kitchen opened. The most beautiful site he could imagine stepped out—Julie!

"Andrew," she said, looking over at his workbench. "Dinner is almost ready." She looked around and saw him in the shadow of the garage light. "Taking a nap before dinner?" she joked.

Andrew struggled to his feet and collapsed to the floor again.

"Andrew!" Julie screamed and ran to him. "What has happened to you? Why are you all muddy and wet? Where have you been?"

"Julie, how many kids do we have?"

"What?' Julie said, "Have you hurt your head?"

"I hurt all over," Andrew replied, "but I need to know. I need you to tell me. I'll explain everything soon."

"We have one child, Andrew. Just like we've always had. Andrew, do I need to call for an ambulance?"

"No. I don't think so," Andrew said. "Just help me up, and let's go inside. I need you to call Matt and Susie and ask them to come over. Please."

Julie thought it was a strange request, but she helped

Andrew inside and called their friends. It didn't take them long to come over, and both expressed their concerns about Andrew and his condition.

"You would have done better to go out with us today," Matt said. "Instead, you stand us up and then get yourself all muddy and beat up by some unknown force."

"It wouldn't have turned out any different, Matt. I'd still be sitting here talking with you. You see, I've been through the scenario where we all went out instead of me working, and I'm still in this position."

"What does that mean, Andrew?" Susie asked.

Andrew looked around and asked, "Does anyone remember anything about our trips in my POD?"

They all looked at each other and were quite confused.

Matt said, "I'd like to hear more about your dream, but it's starting to sound like maybe you woke up next to a pod yourself."

Andrew shook his head and smiled to himself. "I have some amazing things to tell you about our future and things that will happen over the next few months. I will need the help of each of you to make sure that some things don't happen, but in the meantime, we will have an incredible time together, starting next weekend. My friends and family have shown me that they are the best people anyone could ever ask for in the way of friends. I have gone through some events that you might not believe, but you will all witness what I hope will be the best of them. I have notes in my head that I'll be writing down tomorrow. I also want to share all of this with Stephanie when she is a little older. We have so much to do and so much to learn, and I've been given a second chance to get it right. I don't know how much I can change, how much we can change, but I suspect we can make a lot turn out better than it did."

He turned to Julie and said, "While I go up and change and shower, could you make us some hot cocoa? Then, when I come down, I'll tell you all about my weekend adventures and how each of you will play an important part in shaping not only our history but the future history of the world."

Andrew stood on wobbly legs and made his way to the stairs. He turned and looked at his concerned friends. "Get ready for adventures that might spark something hidden in your subconscious. We're going to have fun!"

Born and raised in California, Drew began moving around when he was 14. From California to the East Coast and Texas to Idaho, Drew has seen this country and met its people. He knew he had to begin writing when the stories in his head became so numerous that they had to escape onto paper! He's been published in multiple magazines such as Horseman and Appaloosa News and was the Executive Editor of a sci-fi magazine called Galactic Alliance. This book is Drew's fourth fiction novel. He has also written a book on Bell's Palsy and is currently writing more fiction books you can look forward to reading over the next few years. Drew lives and works in Northern Colorado, where he finds time daily to pursue his writing dreams.